THE MYSTERIOUS FIREPLACE

Books by

CAROLYN KEENE

Nancy Drew Mystery Stories

The Secret of the Old Clock
The Hidden Staircase
The Bungalow Mystery
The Mystery at Lilac Inn
The Secret at Shadow Ranch
The Secret of Red Gate Farm
The Clue in the Diary
Nancy's Mysterious Letter
The Sign of the Twisted Candles
The Password to Larkspur Lane
The Clue of the Broken Locket
The Message in the Hollow Oak
The Mystery of the Ivory Charm
The Whispering Statue
The Haunted Bridge
The Clue of the Tapping Heels
The Mystery of the Brass Bound Trunk
The Mystery at the Moss-Covered Mansion

The Quest of the Missing Map
The Clue in the Jewel Box
The Secret in the Old Attic
The Clue in the Crumbling Wall
The Mystery of the Tolling Bell
The Clue in the Old Album
The Ghost of Blackwood Hall
The Clue of the Leaning Chimney
The Secret of the Wooden Lady
The Clue of the Black Keys
The Mystery at the Ski Jump
The Clue of the Velvet Mask
The Ringmaster's Secret
The Scarlet Slipper Mystery
The Witch Tree Symbol
The Hidden Window Mystery
The Haunted Showboat
The Secret of the Golden Pavilion
The Clue in the Old Stagecoach

Dana Girls Mystery Stories

By the Light of the Study Lamp
The Secret at Lone Tree Cottage
In the Shadow of the Tower
A Three-Cornered Mystery
The Secret at the Hermitage
The Circle of Footprints
The Mystery of the Locked Room
The Clue in the Cobweb
The Secret at the Gatehouse
The Mysterious Fireplace
The Clue of the Rusty Key

The Portrait in the Sand
The Secret in the Old Well
The Clue in the Ivy
The Secret of the Jade Ring
Mystery at the Crossroads
The Ghost in the Gallery
The Clue of the Black Flower
The Winking Ruby Mystery
The Secret of the Swiss Chalet
The Haunted Lagoon
The Mystery of the Bamboo Bird

The DANA GIRLS *Mystery Stories*

THE MYSTERIOUS FIREPLACE

By

CAROLYN KEENE

Grosset & Dunlap, *Publishers*
NEW YORK

Printed in the United States of America

CONTENTS

"Maybe the intruder was after something hidden
in the wall," Louise said at last

The Mysterious Fireplace

CHAPTER I

A Star of Diamonds

"Louise, I have the most exciting news!"

Waving a letter, Jean Dana, her blue eyes alight with eagerness, fairly danced through the open doorway into the cozy dormitory suite she shared with her sister Louise. The two girls were students at Starhurst, a boarding school located near Penfield.

"Louise, didn't you hear me?" Jean demanded as her dark-haired sister scarcely glanced up from the worn, leather-bound volume she had been reading.

"Yes, I heard you," replied Louise dryly. "But I can't believe your news is more exciting than the information I've been learning from this ancient book."

"Oh, you and your books!" scoffed Jean, who was inclined to be less serious than Louise. Although an excellent student, she preferred to devote her spare time to athletics and adventure rather than to the treasures of literature.

1

"Where did you get that musty volume?" she questioned.

She crossed to her sister's study desk, curiously picking up the old book, the title and contents of which were printed in a foreign language. As she fingered through the gilt-edged pages a sheet of paper covered with Louise's notes fluttered to the floor. Jean stooped to pick it up.

"What's this?" she inquired. "A translation?"

"Yes, I've been working on it all afternoon." Louise's face glowed with pride. "I found the book tucked out of sight in one of the locked cases of the library."

"It looks rather dull." Gingerly blond Jean brushed the crumbling leather from her fingers.

"Dull? I've never read anything more fascinating! Why, this volume was published in Europe nearly a hundred years ago. It has been out of print for decades."

"But to spend hours translating it, Louise. Such a job!"

"I don't mind," Louise responded. "It's fascinating. The portion I've worked on tells how many of our Christmas customs came to be. I plan to use the material as a special project in language class. And I have another idea of what to do with it!"

Without giving Jean an opportunity to make

any comments, she hastened on, speaking with increasing enthusiasm.

"You know, Mrs. Crandall asked me to take charge of a series of tableaux for our school Christmas party. Well, the material I've translated from this old volume will provide the basis——"

"All very interesting," interrupted Jean, "but I insist that my news is far more exciting than yours. Of course, if you don't care to hear about what Uncle Ned wrote, it's perfectly all right with me."

"Uncle Ned!" Louise exclaimed, and for the first time her gaze fell upon the envelope in her sister's hand. "Well, why didn't you say you had heard from him!"

"Because you wouldn't give me a chance," Jean laughed.

The letter had been sent from Oak Falls, the town in which the girls made their home with Ned Dana and his maiden sister Harriet. Letters from their uncle were of particular interest because, as captain of the steamship *Balaska*, he traveled to many lands.

"Uncle Ned wrote while at sea," explained Jean. "His message was forwarded by Aunt Harriet, along with one of her own."

"I hope nothing has happened——"

"Oh, no," Jean said reassuringly. "Uncle Ned is safe and so is his ship. The *Balaska* docks in New York tomorrow. But listen to this particular paragraph:

" 'Here is news which should delight my gay, adventure-seeking nieces. Thomas Fair-weather, an old friend of mine, is a passenger aboard the *Balaska*. A few weeks ago he pur-chased an estate on Indian Mountain, a beauti-ful place called Highfort. Now he cordially in-vites us to spend several days there, including Christmas!' "

"Us!" cried Louise. "Does that mean you and me too, Jean?"

"Certainly. That's why I'm so excited. In-dian Mountain, I've heard, is one of the most gorgeous places there is from the standpoint of scenery. Lots of mysterious legends are told about it, too."

"It would be fun to try to track down some of them," said Louise excitedly.

"Oh, we'll have a wonderful Christmas vaca-tion," added Jean. "There's only one thing that worries me and I must admit it has been upsetting."

"What is that?"

"In his letter Uncle Ned says a doctor has ordered him to take a complete rest for at least a week. That was the reason why Mr. Fair-weather extended him the invitation. A moun-tain retreat will be ideal."

"Oh, dear, I hope he's not really ill."

"Just tired, he says. Being captain of a

large steamship naturally is a great responsibility.''

Louise read the entire letter for herself, together with a brief note from Aunt Harriet, who shared their enthusiasm for the proposed trip to Indian Mountain. The mansion at Highfort, she wrote, was a stone house with modern conveniences but once had been a military fort.

''How romantic!'' cried Louise. ''It is probably full of secret passageways and——''

''I wish we were leaving right this minute instead of the end of the week,'' Jean interrupted as she pored over an atlas. ''Let me see, where is Indian Mountain? It should be on this map.''

At that moment a light tap sounded on the door. In response to Louise's greeting, a tall, dark-haired girl timidly entered the room. The Dana sisters recognized her as Sonya Olavu, an attractive foreign student who had entered Starhurst School only a few weeks earlier.

''Am I intruding?'' the girl inquired politely. She spoke slowly, choosing her words with care.

''Not at all,'' replied Jean. ''Have a chair; that is, if you can find one not covered with Louise's books.''

''I shouldn't trouble you, but I am having a difficult time,'' the caller said.

''Has someone been annoying you?'' Jean asked quickly.

She knew that Lettie Briggs, one of the few truly unpleasant students at the school, took delight in making life miserable for the foreign girl. At first the brazen Lettie had forced her attentions upon the newcomer, but the aristocratic Sonya preferred to choose her own companions. Feeling that she had been snubbed, the Briggs girl never missed an opportunity to tease and torment her and held a grudge toward her that showed itself in numerous ways.

"Lettie hasn't bothered me since you and Louise told her she would be reported to the headmistress," Sonya replied. "I feel very grateful to you for having been so kind and helpful."

"Oh, we didn't do anything," Louise laughed. "Lettie can be handled rather easily once you learn her methods."

"I fail to understand a girl of her type, she is so peculiar."

"She's sly and inclined to be jealous," declared Jean. "It bothers her because you are our friend and are not friendly with her."

"Why shouldn't I like you?" Sonya raised wistful brown eyes in a puzzled stare. "You've been so helpful. And now I must call upon you once more to assist me. You must pardon my being so bold."

"Is it an English assignment?" Louise inquired with a smile, for she noted the papers in the girl's hand.

"Yes, I can do nothing with it. The sentences will not come right for me. In my own language I could write smoothly—but in English it makes no sense.''

A sad look came into her eyes, for she was a bit discouraged at the trouble she was having.

''May I see what you have written?'' Louise asked.

Taking the theme from Sonya, Louise read it through and made a number of corrections. She encouraged the girl by declaring that except for minor mistakes the paper was well written.

''You are kind,'' Sonya murmured gratefully. ''Always I ask so many favors of you and Jean, and never am I able to return them.''

''There's something you could do for me,'' said Louise unexpectedly.

''What is it, please?''

''Mrs. Crandall has put me in charge of the Christmas entertainment. An idea came to me this afternoon. I shall try to reproduce famous old paintings!'' Louise declared.

''And you wish me to help sew costumes?'' inquired Sonya, eager to repay the other's kindness.

''No, I need you to take the part of a Madonna. You're exactly the type. You have such a saintly face. Let me see how you'll look draped in white.''

To Sonya's embarrassment Louise seized a sheet and began wrapping it about the girl. Then she stepped back to view her handiwork.

"You'll do," she chuckled. "You'll be given a better costume, of course, and you should have a glittering star to wear just above your forehead. Then you'll look surprisingly like the painting I have in mind."

"Yes, you do fit the part," declared Jean. "You'll be in the entertainment, won't you?"

"Must I speak any lines?"

"Oh, no," explained Louise. "I'll pose you, and you'll keep that position until the footlights are put out. Please say you'll do it."

"Why, yes, if it will help you," Sonya answered willingly. "But I can't believe I resemble a beautiful Madonna."

"You come closer to it than any other girl in the school. And with a brilliant jeweled star to wear——"

"Where can you get such a pin?" Jean inquired dubiously. "I haven't seen any at the stores in Penfield."

"I happen to own a star pin," announced Sonya before Louise could reply. "Shall I get it? I'd love to have you use it."

"Why, yes, if you will," urged Louise gratefully.

Sonya hastened down the hall to her own room, soon returning with a five-pointed star pin which she dropped carelessly into Louise's hand. Sunshine slanting through the windows glinted on the cluster of jewels, causing them to send forth shafts of blue light.

"Sonya, these gems aren't real diamonds?" Louise gasped.

"Oh, yes. The pin is a family heirloom."

"Then it's far too valuable for us to use in the tableau, and too valuable to have in your room."

"But I want you to use it," said Sonya soberly, her lovely eyes glowing. "It might represent also the name of our school. The star of Starhurst."

Jean and Louise were admiring the pin when a maid appeared at the door to say that a caller awaited Sonya in the Red Room downstairs.

"A lady?" asked the foreign girl.

"No, a gentleman, Miss. He gave his name as Mr. Vitescom."

Sonya repeated the name with a quick intake of breath. Although her agitation was evident, she did not speak until the maid had gone. Then she said nervously:

"What shall I do? I know I should see him, but I am afraid."

"Afraid of what?" inquired Jean, puzzled.

Sonya did not reply, giving no indication she had heard the question. Uneasily she fingered the diamond pin Louise had returned to her; then dropped it on the desk. She seemed lost in troubled thought.

"I wish you girls would come with me," she said abruptly. "I am such a coward. I hesitate to face Mr. Vitescom alone."

"We'll be glad to go with you," offered Jean quickly.

"Of course we will," added Louise.

The girls left the suite without closing the door. Neither Jean nor Louise noticed that Sonya did not take the valuable heirloom, which lay on the desk in the Dana suite.

CHAPTER II

The Caller's Claim

Louise and Jean accompanied Sonya down the stairway to the lower floor of the dormitory. Discreetly they waited for her to tell them why she was afraid to see Mr. Vitescom alone.

"He is a disreputable man," the girl explained jerkily. "A blackmailer, you call him in this country."

"You mean he's trying to make you pay him money for some reason?" Jean asked in astonishment.

"Yes, that is it. I blush with shame because he comes from my own country. He has learned certain important secrets of my family."

"You've never told us much about yourself or your people," Louise said encouragingly.

"The past is best forgotten," responded Sonya sadly. "In Europe the Olavu family was known and respected. Then came a bitter day when our tiny country was invaded by enemies. My father was killed, my mother died in a futile attempt to escape to America. Only my older brother and I reached these lovely shores safely."

11

"You have never mentioned your brother before," remarked Jean in surprise.

"I tell you now only because I trust you. If Vitescom and his cohorts should learn Tranley's whereabouts——"

"Tranley is your brother's name?" Jean inquired.

"Yes, he is attending a college not far from here, but under an assumed name. Vitescom has been trying to make me tell him where Tranley can be found. We are fugitives, wanted by the new government which ruthlessly seized our lands. If Tranley were sent back it might be to his death. So you can understand why I am so secretive about things."

"Mr. Vitescom represents the government?"

Sonya shook her head. "No, he is an adventurer, willing to work for whichever side is in power. He pretends to be friends to them and takes their money, but all the time he is working for himself in an underhanded way, I am sure."

"And he has actually threatened you?" Jean questioned, hardly able to believe that this girl was the victim of some plot.

"Indeed, yes. He says that unless I turn over money and certain properties to him he will have my brother deported at once, and I will never see him again."

"He'll have to find him first," remarked Louise grimly, "and I think he never will."

"In some tricky way he will get the truth from

me," Sonya said, pausing at the entrance to one of the dormitory parlors. "I am very much afraid."

"I don't believe you need to be," declared Louise soothingly. "Blackmailers are not tolerated in this country. Why not report him to the police?"

"I'd rather not do that. If the story should appear in the newspapers, both my brother and I might be in danger."

"You could put a private detective on the case," suggested Jean thoughtfully.

"I had considered that, but even so there might be too many questions asked." Sonya hesitated, then added apologetically, "Everyone has told me about the marvelous work you two girls have accomplished in solving mysteries. I wish—but no, it is too much to ask."

Louise and Jean Dana exchanged questioning glances. Obviously Sonya was eager to have them take an active part in her tangled affairs, and the prospect was not displeasing to them. Unusual people, odd facts, strange settings never failed to arouse their interest—traits which explained why mystery and adventure so frequently came into their lives.

Louise and Jean were orphans, who for many years had shared the Oak Falls home of their maiden aunt, Harriet Dana, and their Uncle Ned. The household was a happy one, made amusing by the mishaps of Cora Appel, a loyal but slow-witted maid of all work whom **Jean** teasingly had nicknamed "Applecore."

The Dana girls were leaders at their school, which was supervised by Professor and Mrs. Crandall. There Louise and Jean had made many friends and had enjoyed experiences unusual to students of their age.

Recently they had been guests at the Warrington estate a few miles away. It pleased them to recall that their friendship with Evangeline Warrington had resulted in their solving a strange mystery in connection with "The Secret at the Gatehouse."

Louise and Jean thoroughly enjoyed fitting together clues to bring about the solution of puzzling cases. A curious tower, an abandoned country home, a western ranch—each had provided an intriguing setting for their sleuthing abilities. Now, at the thought that they might be of assistance to Sonya, they were aware of a subdued feeling of excitement.

"You know we'll be glad to aid you in any way we can, Sonya," Louise said in a low-pitched voice. "What is it that you hesitate to ask?"

"I should rather have you and Louise protecting me than any detective I could ever employ," the girl announced.

"That is very flattering," said Jean, "and Louise and I feel very highly complimented."

As she spoke, a flush of pleasure spread over her face.

"We'll try to see that Mr. Vitescom doesn't annoy you," Louise declared, starting determinedly forward. "Where is he, I wonder?"

Jean caught her sister's hand, detaining her.

"Wait, Louise. Vitescom never will admit anything in our presence. If we hope to learn his little game we should allow Sonya to talk with him alone. Only in that way can we get the whole truth."

"That's so," Louise admitted. "I have it! We can enter one of the empty parlors, hide behind the velvet draperies, and have Sonya bring her caller into that room."

"How does the idea appeal to you?" Jean asked, turning to the foreign girl.

"I won't be afraid if I am sure you are near. It will help me to know that my friends are standing by."

"First, let's have a peep at Mr. Vitescom," proposed Louise. "The maid said he was in the Red Room. I can hardly wait to see him."

Passing through a deserted parlor, the three girls approached the entrance to the adjoining room. From the doorway they were able to see a tall, slender, dark man who stood at the window, his face in profile. He was well dressed; his appearance gave no indication that he was not the suave and polished gentleman he seemed to be. His hair was neatly combed, his shoes highly polished, and he carried an expensive looking overcoat on his arm.

"Is that Vitescom?" whispered Jean.

"Yes," returned Sonya, very low. "But don't be deceived. He's cruel and mean."

"Jean and I will hide in this room," Louise instructed. "Make some excuse to bring your caller here. Then encourage him to talk."

"He will do that without encouragement," returned Sonya bitterly. "I have never met a man so sinister—he terrifies me."

"Don't let him know you are afraid," Louise advised. "And remember, we'll be right here should you need our help."

The Dana girls secreted themselves behind the velvet draperies at the window and waited. With great reluctance Sonya went to meet Mr. Vitescom.

Louise and Jean heard a steady murmur of voices which grew plainer as the couple approached from the other room. To their chagrin they could not understand a word of the conversation. Sonya and Mr. Vitescom were speaking in a foreign language.

The couple took seats not far from where the Dana girls were hiding. The two sisters felt relieved to hear Sonya say in English:

"Let us continue our discussion in the tongue of my adopted land, Mr. Vitescom."

"Adopted land—bah!" the foreigner exclaimed. He spoke with a pronounced accent. "You and your brother are not Americans. You try to forget your native country. But your country does not forget you and how you ran away with a fortune of jewels! No!"

"My brother and I took only what belonged to our family," Sonya retorted indignantly.

"You disobeyed one of the new laws. It says you cannot take them here."

"The law was made after my brother and I had fled."

Vitescom edged closer to Sonya and began speaking in his own language again. His voice rose to a higher pitch. Jean and Louise easily guessed that he was threatening the girl with some unpleasant fate.

"No! No!" she cried wildly, cringing away. "I shall never tell you where you can find my brother! And you shall never have the jewels! You would sell them for yourself or turn them over to the evil ones who hired you to come here."

Louise and Jean listened alertly to every word. Although they could not understand what Vitescom was saying, it was fairly clear to them that Sonya must have valuable jewels in her possession. Probably the beautiful star pin was part of the collection! Was the girl hiding the jewels somewhere at Starhurst School?

As Sonya dared to defy him, the man's anger was fanned to white heat. Grasping the girl's wrists, he pressed his cheek almost against hers as a torrent of words poured into her ear.

Until that moment Sonya had faced her tormentor with courage. Now, however, she seemed to wilt beneath his wrath. She appeared incapable of answering his threats and her face was so pale the Dana girls feared she was going to faint.

"We can't allow this to go on," Louise whispered to Jean. "Let's do something about it."

Pushing aside the velvet curtains, they stepped out to confront Mr. Vitescom. Jean gave the man a little push away from the trembling Sonya, while Louise placed a protecting arm about her.

"So! You listen behind the curtain!" the man exclaimed in English. "You are spies!"

"We are friends of Sonya," Jean corrected him sternly. "We'll not stand quietly by and see her abused by you or anyone else."

Her words served to send the man into another tirade. So loudly did he shout that Mrs. Crandall came hurrying from an adjoining room.

"Dear me," she murmured, gazing from one to the other, "is something wrong?"

Louise and Jean explained what had occurred. Their story was supported by Sonya and angrily denied by Mr. Vitescom. His red face and gasping tones caused the headmistress to form her own opinion of the situation. Po-

litely but firmly she asked him to leave and not
to call again at the dormitory.

"I am so sorry, Mrs. Crandall," Sonya apologized sorrowfully after the man had gone. "I
have caused what you call a scene. You would
like me to leave the school forever?"

"Certainly not, Sonya," the headmistress replied. "It wasn't your fault that Mr. Vitescom
came here. I only regret that I was unable to
protect you. His appearance must have deceived the maid into thinking he was a friend."

Sonya felt greatly relieved and was quite
cheerful as she climbed the stairs with Jean and
Louise. She was inclined to think that Vitescom never would trouble her again, an opinion
the Dana girls could not share.

The door to Lettie Briggs's room stood
slightly ajar. As the three girls walked past,
she was talking in a loud voice to her roommate,
Ina Mason, saying that she planned to spend the
Christmas holidays at a wonderful mountain
lodge.

"Father and I will hunt big game," she
stated grandly. "I expect to shoot several
bears and have their skins made into rugs for
our room. Oh, it's a wild place, but the lodge
has every modern convenience and a host of
servants."

Jean would have paid no heed to such talk,
for it was well known that Lettie Briggs frequently made up stories, but something else

caught her attention. Before she had gone far down the hall she heard another snatch of conversation which alarmed her.

"I saw them in the parlor downstairs," Lettie was saying, "and they were having a frightful fuss. I guess she's a thief."

Jean glanced quickly at Sonya and Louise. Neither appeared to have heard the remark. Without telling them of her intention, she dropped a few paces behind. After they had disappeared she quietly entered Lettie's room.

"I knew it was a mistake when Mrs. Crandall allowed that girl Sonya to come here," Lettie was telling Ina. "If you could have heard that man yelling at her——"

"Excuse me," said Jean coldly.

"Oh, it's you!" Lettie broke off and a flush painted her cheeks.

"I couldn't help hearing. Lettie, you shouldn't say things about Sonya which are not true. That caller is no friend of hers, and she's not a thief!"

"Then he was threatening her. She must have done something wrong or he wouldn't have been so angry."

"Sonya has done nothing wrong. You aren't being fair to start such a story."

"Who is starting anything?" Lettie Briggs demanded defiantly.

"You were telling Ina things which aren't true."

"I was only telling her what I saw with my own eyes," said the other defiantly.

"That's so," added Ina, bobbing her head.

"Well, don't spread such tales about Sonya or you'll be sorry," Jean repeated, fire in her eye.

Actually, she had little confidence in Lettie, and would have had far less had she overheard the conversation which took place immediately after her departure.

"Jean thinks she can tell *me* what to do," Lettie said indignantly. "Why, the very idea!"

"Bossy, isn't she?" prodded Ina, always eager to get Lettie to talk so as to get information.

Jean opened the door of her own suite. Both Sonya and Louise were there, and she noticed instantly that something was amiss. The room was in disorder, and the two girls were frantically searching the wastepaper basket.

"Why, what's wrong?" asked Jean in astonishment.

"My star pin!" Sonya answered unsteadily, a frown creasing her smooth brow. "I left it here on the desk. Now we can't find it anywhere."

CHAPTER III

The Surprise Gift

"Why, Sonya!" exclaimed Jean, dismayed at the news. "I thought you took the diamond pin with you when we went downstairs."

"No, I left it lying on the desk," Sonya answered, emptying paper from the wastebasket. "Louise thought it might have fallen off, but it's not on the floor or here."

"How valuable is the pin?"

"Our family never placed a price upon it. I should think it would be worth five thousand dollars at least."

The Dana girls gasped.

"Sonya, you should have taken better care of it," Louise said in a worried tone. "We didn't even lock the door."

"It never occurred to me anyone would steal it—not at Starhurst."

"I can't believe such a thing myself," admitted Jean, "but one can't be too careful. Let me help search. Perhaps I can find it."

With a broom from the hall closet she went carefully over the floor, but the pin was not found. Nor were there any clues to disclose whether or not the room had been entered during their absence.

At that moment a friend of the Dana girls, named Evelyn, came down the hall.

"Anything wrong?" she inquired, pausing in the open doorway.

Quickly the girls explained about the pin and its mysterious disappearance.

"Did you see anyone in this hall during the past twenty minutes?" Louise questioned her, hoping for a clue.

"No strangers. Lettie and Ina were up here to see one of the girls."

"They didn't enter this room?"

"Not while I was watching."

"Lettie is sly but she isn't dishonest," said Jean thoughtfully. "I can't believe she would steal the pin."

"We must tell Mrs. Crandall," declared Louise in a discouraged tone. "There's nothing else to do."

"I hope my other jewels are safe," Sonya commented nervously, clasping and unclasping her hands.

"Your other jewels!" Louise's eyes opened wide. "Sonya, have you really been keeping a collection of valuable gems in your bedroom?"

"Oh, I hid them in a safe place. And the door is locked."

Louise and Jean were alarmed lest a professional thief had entered the dormitory and had stolen the entire cache. Upon hastening with Sonya to her room they were relieved to find that the jewels—a leather case filled with rings, bracelets, necklaces and odd pieces—remained safely hidden in her clothes closet.

"You're lucky they are still here," declared Louise severely. "Sonya, please promise me that you'll put your valuables in a bank deposit vault."

Sonya's answer was discouraging. "I don't trust banks, because our family lost a great deal of money when one failed. But I promise that during the holidays I'll find a safer place."

No amount of persuasion on the part of the Danas could make her change her mind. Although disturbed by her loss, Sonya said little about it, feeling that Jean and Louise might blame themselves. It was the sisters who went to Mrs. Crandall with the story of the theft.

"Unquestionably, the pin has been stolen," the headmistress declared. "I am distressed that such a thing should happen, even though Sonya was unwise to bring expensive jewelry with her to the school."

Louise and Jean discussed every angle of the puzzling affair with Mrs. Crandall. However, they avoided mentioning Lettie Briggs's name. They had no proof she had entered their room, and could not believe that the girl would stoop to such a dishonorable act.

"Oh, by the way, Louise," Mrs. Crandall commented as the Dana girls were leaving the office, "how are you progressing with plans for the Christmas entertainment?"

"Rehearsals start tomorrow," Louise assured her. "My ideas aren't fully developed yet, but in another day I hope to have a program ready for your approval."

During the remainder of the afternoon the Dana girls looked over the ancient book which Louise had found in the library. They came upon many pictures showing interesting old Christmas customs.

"These would make wonderful tableaux," said Jean enthusiastically to Louise as they turned the pages.

"Listen to this," commanded Louise, completing a translation. "I'll bet few people know how the custom of filling stockings at Christmas time began.

" 'In the Middle Ages a fine old man named Nicholas, who later became a Saint, decided he would give a present to each of the poor peasants in his neighborhood on Christmas Eve. As he was doing it in the real spirit of Christmas, he did not want his deed known. Realizing that at night the peasant men, after removing their heavy boots, always hung up their socks in front of the fire to dry, Nicholas thought of a way to carry out what he wanted to do. At midnight he cautiously descended the stone steps in the chimneys and dropped a gold piece into the toe of each stocking while the owner slept.

" 'For years he continued the practice without anyone guessing his secret. Peoples in many countries heard the story and gave the kindly old saint a name of their own. He began to be called Santa Claus and other titles and more and more legends and customs grew up about him.' "

"Say, Louise, couldn't you make that into a tableau?" asked Jean. "Use the scene where Santa Claus drops a piece of gold into each sock hanging by the fireplace!"

"I was thinking of it. Maybe we could get Old Terry, the school bus driver, to take the part of Santa Claus!"

"That reminds me, Louise. Lettie Briggs has been hinting that you won't give her a part in the entertainment. She says you have a grudge against her."

"How silly!"

"Lettie never takes a part well. If I were you I'd forget her."

"No, I have a role for her," Louise chuckled. "Be sure to tell her to come to the gymnasium tomorrow evening for rehearsal."

Jean carried the message to the Briggs girl who appeared thrilled by the invitation. That night at dinner she boasted that she had been given the leading part in the Christmas entertainment. The Dana girls did not correct her.

The following evening the gymnasium was filled with students by the time Lettie arrived.

"Sorry to be late," she flung indifferently at the chairman. "Where's the costume I am to wear?"

Louise pointed to a ragged robe lying on a near-by chair.

"What! That old thing!" Lettie fairly shrieked. "You don't expect me to wear a mess of rags! I'd look like a beggar in them!"

"You're to take the part of a poor ragged shepherd, Lettie. You'll carry a toy lamb in your arms," said Louise.

"Oh no I won't!" snapped Lettie. "I won't be in your stupid old entertainment. I'll have a good part or none at all."

"Just as you please."

Followed by the amused glances of the other students, Lettie fled from the room. The rehearsal was resumed in a few minutes.

Everyone agreed that Louise had shown excellent judgment in selecting Sonya for the Madonna character. Worried by the loss of the diamond pin, she seemed more than ever suited to the part, her face having assumed a sad, sweet expression.

During the days which followed both Jean and Louise were kept so busy that they had no time to take up the search for the lost jewel. Together they fashioned a homemade star to be worn by Sonya in the tableau. It was a poor substitute for the original ornament, however.

Frequently the Dana girls discussed the mysterious theft, but they could arrive at no definite conclusions. Without a single clue they held scant hope of tracing the missing property.

"I'll always believe someone living in the dormitory took the pin," declared Jean gloomily. "But Mrs. Crandall has had no better luck than we in discovering the guilty person."

The annual school entertainment had been scheduled for an evening a few days hence. Louise and Jean packed their traveling bags the afternoon before. That left their final day at Starhurst free to help in decorating the halls with balsam and holly, attending to last-minute arrangements for the entertainment, and for the party which would come just ahead of it.

"This Christmas party will be the nicest our school has ever had," Jean said gaily as she stood on tiptoes to tie an ornament on a high branch of a glittering evergreen tree in the reception room.

"I surely hope so," replied Louise soberly. "Everything has been carefully planned, but I have an uneasy feeling. Lettie is provoked at me and I don't trust her. There is something wrong somewhere."

Despite her own misgiving, events moved smoothly throughout the day. Following an excellent dinner, the school orchestra played several selections, poetry was read, and carols were sung. Then the girls gathered in the parlor for the distribution of gifts. A giant log glowed on the open hearth, and the brilliant lights of the Christmas tree were reflected in the happy eyes of the students.

One by one, Mrs. Crandall presented the tissue-wrapped presents from the tree. Several days before the girls had drawn names, purchasing dollar gifts for one another. These were opened with great merriment. The last package, removed from the far side of the tree, bore Sonya's name.

"But this is a mistake," the girl protested. "I've already received one gift. Why should I receive two?"

"Nevertheless, it's for you," said Jean. "Do open it."

As Sonya removed the gold ribbon, two pieces of cardboard fell to the floor, together with a sealed envelope. There was nothing more.

"What can it be?" Sonya asked, deeply mystified.

She stooped and picked up the envelope. With the girls gathered about her, she tore it open. Inside lay a ten-dollar bill and a yellow slip of paper which bore printing.

"Why, it's a pawn ticket!" exclaimed Louise, leaning forward to see better.

"But I've pawned nothing," said Sonya in bewilderment. "Why was it sent to me?"

"I think I know!" cried Jean. "I'll bet that

the person who took your diamond pin pawned it at this Penfield shop!"

"And sent you this ticket because his conscience hurt him," added Louise quickly. "Oh, if only we had the star so that you could wear it for the tableau."

Jean turned pleading eyes upon the headmistress. "Mrs. Crandall, may I go to Penfield now and investigate? Old Terry could take me in the school bus. I think I could get back within half an hour."

The headmistress hesitated, then gave her consent.

"Do hurry, Jean," Louise urged her sister in a whisper. "If you're late in getting back with Terry, the entertainment will be ruined."

"It won't take me long," promised Jean.

The girls saw her drive away in the bus. For a time there was a lot of buzzing among the students regarding the lost pin. Then as the school orchestra began to play Christmas music, conversation ceased and the girls went into the auditorium.

Nervously Louise watched the clock. A half hour elapsed and Jean had not returned. It was time for the tableaux, and Old Terry was to take the part of Santa Claus in the very first one. Without him it would have no significance. Already the students were squirming restlessly in their chairs.

Evelyn moved quietly to Louise's side.

"Don't you think we should start?" she urged in a whisper. "I'm afraid the girls won't remain patient much longer."

"I know, but what can I do? I need both Terry and Jean. I can't understand it," Louise said miserably. "I'm afraid they've had an accident."

CHAPTER IV

AN UNEXPLAINED DELAY

THE minutes dragged slowly on and still Jean and old Terry did not return. Sonya and Mrs. Crandall both shared Louise's alarm. Presently the headmistress went to her office, there to telephone to the Penfield pawnshop.

Receiving no answer, she called Mr. Goldman at his home. From the owner of the place she learned that Jean had left the store more than half an hour earlier. She had the diamond pin in her possession.

"Then she did obtain it!" exclaimed Louise when told of the conversation.

"Yes," nodded Mrs. Crandall, "but why isn't Jean here? She has had ample time to make the trip."

Another twenty minutes elapsed. The student audience became increasingly impatient. Lettie Briggs, thoroughly pleased that Louise was uncomfortable, whispered loudly that the real reason for the delay was because certain stage properties had failed to arrive. Encouraged by her, Ina Mason and two other girls left the auditorium.

Mrs. Crandall might have taken charge of

matters had she not been busy at the telephone. Fearful lest harm had overtaken Jean she called the Penfield police station. She requested that a search be made for the missing school bus and its two occupants.

"Louise, you must start the program," Evelyn urged her friend. "Unless you do, the entire audience may leave."

"But I need Terry for the part of Santa Claus in the first tableau."

"If he doesn't get here, I'll take it," responded Evelyn. "I know exactly what to do."

Thus encouraged, Louise stood up and faced the audience. She began to speak in a carefully controlled voice which gave no hint of her great worry about her sister.

" 'In olden times, when there was no heat in houses except from fireplaces, family life centered around these important places in the homes. Here the cooking and clothes drying were done and in the evenings games were played and stories were told.' "

Making use of ancient source material, Louise went on to relate how the custom of hanging up stockings had originated in peasant homes and finally became a Christmas custom throughout much of the world.

"We see such a cottage now," she said, drawing the velvet curtains aside.

Louise held her breath, feeling almost certain that the first tableau would give cause for laughter rather than admiration. She need have had no such fear.

Behind a giant picture frame, which Terry had fashioned with much care, was a lifelike portrayal of Saint Nicholas dropping gold coins into socks hung up at a fireplace. Evelyn, as the old saint, kept her face slightly turned. She held the pose perfectly until Louise dropped the curtain.

"Again! Again!" chorused the delighted audience, clapping loudly.

Louise hesitated. Then, hoping to gain additional time, she obligingly obeyed.

Evelyn stood as quietly as before but for only a moment. Suddenly a mouse scurried across the floor almost at her feet. Saint Nicholas gave a little jump which caused the students to rock with laughter.

> " 'Twas the night before Christmas
> And all through the house——"

warbled Lettie, who had come back to her seat.

Louise flushed, and an angry glint came into her eyes. Above the good-natured chuckles of the girls she had heard another sound—a snicker which proved that someone was at the hall doorway just beyond the stage. Turning her head quickly she caught a flash of blue silk.

"Ina Mason!" she thought. "That girl deliberately brought in the mouse! And I'll bet

Lettie put her up to it. She *would* do a thing like that!''

Hiding her annoyance, Louise went on with the program. There were no further disturbances, for even Lettie Briggs became interested as one Christmas picture after another was presented in tableau. The audience applauded vigorously, demanding that many of the scenes be repeated.

After a few minutes Mrs. Crandall re-entered the auditorium, taking a seat on the front row. Louise glanced directly at the headmistress, asking a question with her eyes. The woman inclined her head slightly in negative answer. Jean had not been found.

''Oh, I'm afraid something dreadful has happened to her,'' thought Louise with a sinking heart.

Courageously she went on with her talk, but did so with a heavy heart. It was nearing time for the final tableau, the Madonna scene which would feature Sonya.

Suddenly there was a little stir in the room as a maid tiptoed down the aisle and paused beside Mrs. Crandall's chair. She whispered something to the headmistress, who nodded and immediately followed the girl from the auditorium.

For a moment Louise's voice wavered. She felt that she could not go on with the program. Something had happened to Jean; of that she was absolutely certain. What mattered a mere entertainment? She must learn the truth at once about her sister.

Then a second inner voice told her that she must see the program through to the end. Mrs. Crandall expected it of her.

Regaining control of herself, Louise quietly explained the significance of the final tableau. At the proper moment she pulled aside the velvet curtains slowly.

A gasp of astonishment and delight came from the audience. Louise held her breath at what she saw. There was Sonya, kneeling in her snow-white robes, more beautiful than any-one ever had seen her. In her hair, just above her forehead, gleamed a brilliant five-pointed star pin!

Louise rubbed her eyes, wondering if she were dreaming. But there could be no mistake. The pin which Sonya wore was her own .

The girls clapped enthusiastically, demand-ing that the curtain be raised many times. At last, however, they were satisfied, and the en-tertainment ended with everyone except Lettie declaring that it had been a great success. Louise, though being praised on all sides, lost not a minute in hastening to the dressing room.

"Sonya!" she cried joyfully. "Your pin has been recovered!"

"Yes," the lovely girl replied, her eyes shining with happiness. "It was sent by messenger to Mrs. Crandall."

"Where is Jean?"

The headmistress, who had been standing near, moved toward Louise. She placed an arm about the girl's shoulder.

"Now please don't be alarmed," she said gently. "I am sure everything will come out all right."

"Something has happened to Jean!"

"Your sister has been in a little accident, I am afraid. Unfortunately, I haven't learned the details——"

"Where is she?" Louise asked frantically. "Where is Jean now?"

"In the Penfield hospital," Mrs. Crandall responded soberly. "We shall go there at once."

CHAPTER V

Jean's Mishap

As a taxicab carried them toward Penfield, Mrs. Crandall explained to Louise how Sonya's pin had come into her possession.

"A policeman brought it to the school in Jean's purse," she revealed. "He left before I had an opportunity to question him."

"Then you don't know whether or not Jean is seriously injured?" cried Louise.

"The only information I have was relayed to me by the maid. The officer told her that your sister had urged him to rush the star of diamonds to the school as it was needed for the entertainment."

"When was the message given, I wonder?"

"Just as Jean was being admitted to the hospital, I believe."

Mrs. Crandall's words could not fail to alarm Louise. Although the headmistress kept reassuring her that everything would be all right, the older Dana girl was greatly worried about her sister. Her relief was great, therefore, when upon reaching the hospital she was told that Jean was in no danger.

"It was only a minor accident," the woman at the desk said with a smile. "You may see her now, if you wish. Room 408."

An elevator carried Mrs. Crandall and Louise to the fourth floor. They wandered down a long hall until they came to the indicated room, where they paused a moment. The door was open. Jean was sitting up in bed, her head and left arm neatly bandaged. A roguish smile lighted up her pretty face.

"Oh, hello," she greeted the callers cheerfully. "Did you get the pin in time for the tableau?"

"We certainly did," Louise answered heartily. "Jean, what has happened? You and Terry were in a motor accident?"

"Nothing of the sort," grinned Jean. "Terry didn't tell you the story?"

"We've not seen him," said Mrs. Crandall. "I do hope your injuries aren't bad. This is very, very serious."

"Mere scratches," laughed Jean carelessly. "I got them in a scuffle with Mr. Vitescom. Please don't think I'm hurt badly, for I'm not."

"Vitescom!" exclaimed Louise, wondering if she had heard right. "You didn't meet him, did you?"

"Oh, didn't I?" Jean waved her sister and Mrs. Crandall into chairs beside the bed. "Let me tell you I've had a real adventure."

"I should not have permitted you to set off with only Terry as an escort," the worried head-mistress said self-accusingly.

"Oh, Terry was splendid. But he's not a very fast runner."

Jean chuckled at the vivid recollection, then plunged into her story.

"Terry and I drove directly to the pawnshop after we left Starhurst. We found the place closed, so we went to Mr. Goldman's home. When I showed him the pawn ticket he said at once that the diamond pin had been deposited with him for ten dollars."

"Who pawned it?" Louise interrupted.

"A girl named Maggie Marsh. I wonder who she can be?"

"We have no one by that name in our school," commented Mrs. Crandall. "This is indeed strange."

"I had never heard of her either," resumed Jean. "Anyway, Mr. Goldman went back to the shop with me and got the pin from the safe. Then Terry and I started to drive back to the school. That was when the fun began."

"What happened?" asked Louise, reaching over to smooth a blanket on Jean's bed.

"Just at the edge of town Terry had to stop for a traffic light. Suddenly a man jerked open the car door. My, what a shock that was!"

"Not Vitescom?"

"Yes, it was, Louise. I recognized him even

in the poor light. He must have been watching
what happened at the pawnshop, for he snatched
my handbag and fled.''

"Knowing you as I do, I can guess that you
ran after him,'' said Louise, smiling faintly
and wishing she might have been there.

"Certainly I did. Terry was with me for
about twenty yards. Then he became winded.''

"Oh, Jean,'' murmured Mrs. Crandall, "you
never should have pursued that dreadful man.''

"I couldn't let him steal Sonya's pin. With
all the strength I had I ran after Vitescom and
finally overtook him. I seized my handbag and
screamed for help. When Vitescom saw a policeman coming, he ran off. But first he gave me
a push which sent me over backwards, and I
struck the ground full force.''

"That was how you were hurt?'' Louise inquired.

"Yes, I went down hard, but I held fast to
the handbag,'' she smiled.

"Jean, you are very courageous but reck-
less,'' Mrs. Crandall chided the girl. "However, I haven't the heart to scold you, for you
saved Sonya's valuable pin.''

"And the tableau as well,'' added Louise
gratefully. "Thanks to you, the entertainment
was a great success.''

"I'm glad everything turned out well,'' said
Jean, weariness in her voice. "It makes all my
aches and pains worth while.''

"I wonder what became of Terry?" mused Mrs. Crandall.

"He was so winded I'm sure he had to stop and rest," replied Jean. "By the time he got his breath I probably was gone. Maybe he's still hunting for me!"

"How did you get to the hospital?" Louise asked her sister.

"Oh, the policeman who arrived insisted. He was too late to catch Vitescom but he hailed a passing car and brought me here. Silly, wasn't it?"

"Quite the contrary," responded Mrs. Crandall. "While I haven't talked with the doctor, I feel convinced that you will require absolute quiet for a few days."

"Quiet?" Jean wailed. "Oh, no! Why, Aunt Harriet is expecting Louise and me at Oak Falls tomorrow! We're driving to Indian Mountain for a grand Christmas!"

"I hope you will be able to go," said the headmistress soothingly. "We'll see in the morning. You must try to sleep now."

A few minutes later Mrs. Crandall and Louise left the hospital, satisfied that Jean would have the best of care. They were relieved by a doctor's assurance that the girl's injuries had been slight. In all probability she would be able to return to the dormitory the next day.

"Even so, this means that Jean and I cannot start for Oak Falls in the morning," Louise remarked anxiously. "I must telephone to Aunt Harriet without delay."

Although the hour was late, she placed a long distance call immediately upon her return to Starhurst School. Miss Dana's somewhat sleepy voice came to her through the receiver.

"Hello, is it you, Louise? I was in bed when the phone rang."

"I'm sorry to disturb you, Aunt Harriet," Louise apologized, and then quickly related what had occurred. "We can't come home tomorrow. Couldn't you drive to Penfield and pick up Jean and me in the car, say day after tomorrow?"

"Of course," agreed Miss Dana instantly. "You're sure Jean is all right?"

"Oh, she'll be as well as ever in a day or so," Louise replied. "Her little mishap shouldn't interfere with our trip to Indian Mountain."

There was a slight pause before Miss Dana said, "Louise, you mustn't be too disappointed if we don't go."

"Oh, Aunt Harriet! Jean really isn't hurt badly——"

"It's not that, Louise. Your Uncle Ned arrived this afternoon with his friend Mr. Fairweather. It seems there has been some trouble about the estate. Mr. Fairweather has been unable to get a clear title to the Indian Mountain property, so he doesn't really own it yet. Unless he has favorable news soon we'll probably spend Christmas at Oak Falls."

"Oh, I see," murmured Louise, disappointment in her voice.

"We'll have a nice time, anyway," finished Aunt Harriet with forced good cheer. "You may look for us to drive to Penfield no later than day after tomorrow."

With a heavy heart Louise went to her room and to bed. The suite seemed very empty and lonely without Jean. From near-by rooms she could hear laughter and talking as the students packed their belongings for the holidays they looked forward to so eagerly.

By the time Louise awakened the next morning the dormitory was nearly deserted of students. In an attempt to keep herself occupied, she ate breakfast slowly, then returned to her room and sat down at her desk. She began to translate a few more pages of the fascinating volume about Christmas customs. The particular passage which she had selected described certain early fireplaces used by European peasants and also by pioneers in our own country.

"Frequently there were steps built into these huge stone fireplaces which led to the roof of the cottage," she read. "In very cold weather or in case of attack by an enemy, windows were barricaded and ventilation as well as means of entrance and exit was through the chimney."

The information intrigued Louise, but before she could translate further a light tap sounded on the door.

"Come in," she invited cordially.

Sonya stood in the doorway, her coat and hat on. She had come to express her appreciation for the recovery of the diamond pin and to inquire about Jean's condition.

"I telephoned to the hospital this morning early," Louise told the girl, offering a chair. "Jean is feeling well and will be brought here some time today."

"I am so happy to hear it," Sonya said. She extended two tiny, tissue-wrapped packages. "This one is for you, Louise. Please give the other to Jean when she comes."

"Dear me, you haven't brought us Christmas gifts!"

"They are nothing. Only a small token of friendship, that's all."

Louise removed the tissue paper and ribbon. Disclosed was a dainty, old-fashioned jeweled bouquet clasp in the form of two pansies.

"Jean's is the same except that the flowers are roses," explained Sonya. "The clasps have been in our family for several generations."

"But, Sonya," Louise protested, "these beautiful pins are heirlooms. You shouldn't give them away to anybody."

"It is as I wish," smiled Sonya. "Please accept the gifts."

Realizing that the friendly giver would be hurt by a refusal, Louise graciously thanked her and accepted the clasps. As the caller turned to leave, the Dana girl casually inquired regarding her vacation plans.

"I depart in a few minutes," Sonya answered. "My brother and I will be together for the holidays."

"I hope you have a Merry Christmas," said Louise. "And do relieve my mind by taking good care of your family jewels."

Sonya's brown eyes danced with amusement, then she became serious. "I have them locked in my suitcase now."

"You don't intend to carry them around with you during the holidays!" exclaimed Louise.

"Oh, no," chuckled Sonya, "my brother and I will put them in a safe place."

"I'm glad to hear that. You mean a bank vault, I assume?"

Sonya shook her head as she retreated through the open door. "My brother and I know of a better place," she replied. "In a mysterious fireplace!"

With that she was gone, leaving Louise to stare after her in complete bewilderment.

CHAPTER VI

The Sleepwalker

Louise decided to employ the morning trying to find out who Maggie Marsh, the girl who pawned the star pin, might be. She would call at the hospital and talk over the matter with Jean.

"Hello!" the younger girl cried as Louise entered her room. "I'd like to get up and go home but the doctor won't let me," she pretended to pout.

"Never mind," her sister consoled her. "You can be doing something useful even if you have to stay in bed."

Louise now launched upon her idea of tracing Maggie Marsh. At once Jean became interested, forgetting her own disappointment. She offered several bits of helpful advice, which Louise would follow.

"Well, good-bye, honey," the older girl said as she assured herself that Jean really was practically well.

"Farewell, sleuth," her sister waved.

Louise's first stop was the Goldman Pawn-shop to learn what she could about the person who had brought Sonya's pin there. The owner answered all her questions willingly, but he could give her no useful description of the girl who had called herself Maggie Marsh.

"She wore a dark nose veil which hid her eyes," he explained. "Her voice was high-pitched. That's about all I remember."

Louise now inquired at several places in Penfield; stores, the beauty shop and the hotels. She even examined a directory. No one had heard of Maggie Marsh and her name was not listed as a resident.

"It's my guess the pin was pawned by someone who used an assumed name," the Dana girl decided at last.

Wearily she turned back to Starhurst, depressed that she had not solved the mystery. The only bright thought was that at least Sonya had the valuable heirloom again.

Early the next morning Jean was brought from the hospital, and began talking of the trip to Indian Mountain. Louise was forced to relay Aunt Harriet's message.

"Matters could be a whole lot worse, though," she declared to her sister. "You're feeling well again, and we'll manage to have a pleasant holiday. There are lots of parties we can go to."

Late that afternoon two automobiles arrived from Oak Falls. Jean, who was at a parlor window, saw her aunt, Uncle Ned and Cora Appel alight from one, and a portly gentleman from the other.

"They've come!" she shouted joyously to Louise. "Oh, I guess we're going to that intriguing sounding estate after all!"

The girls ran to the door to greet the visitors. Aunt Harriet inquired anxiously about Jean, and then introduced Thomas Fairweather, the Danas' guest. Although he was a man well past middle age, he was athletic looking and had a jolly manner which delighted the young people.

"So these are the girls you've told me about, Ned," he said heartily. "Well, you're a lucky man to have them for nieces. I'd like that myself. Maybe, young ladies," he added, a twinkle in his eyes, "you'll call me Uncle Tom?"

The sisters laughed and promised to remember his request.

"Well, well!" the man said, gazing about the great pine-studded hall. "You have a very comfortable place here. But you're going to like the mansion at Indian Mountain even better."

Louise and Jean gazed quickly toward their aunt and uncle. "Indian Mountain!" they exclaimed in unison, and Jean added, "Are we actually going?"

"Aye, that we are," boomed Captain Dana. "Just as soon as we can stow your luggage in the hold, we'll be on our way!"

"Don't forget your skis," Mr. Fairweather reminded the girls. "You'll find plenty of snow at Indian Mountain."

Cora Appel accompanied the girls upstairs

that she might see their suite and help them with their luggage. They found her to be even more absent-minded than usual. She brushed a bottle of ink from Louise's desk and reached for a dress of Jean's with which to wipe up the stain.

"Don't! Don't!" shrieked the younger Dana girl, darting forward to save the frock.

"Oh, lawsy me," the maid gasped. "I dunno what's wrong with me today. I can't keep my mind on what I'm a-doin'."

"You are rather dreamy-eyed," Louise commented as she helped Jean wipe the floor. "Not in love again, I hope?"

The Dana girls delighted in teasing Cora about her many boy friends. Yet each new "case" was a great trial to the Dana family, for experience had proven that the silly girl could do little work while in the midst of a romance.

"Oh, I ain't in love," Cora tittered self-consciously. "But Jenkins is jest real nice. The nicest man I ever saw in all my life."

"Jenkins?" Jean caught her up. "Now who in the world is he?"

"He drives the auto for Mr. Fairweather. You can see him from the window." Cora pointed to one of the cars parked on the driveway. "Ain't he handsome in his uniform and those leather things around his legs?"

Jean looked at her sister in despair. She and Louise were afraid that on the trip to Indian

Mountain the maid might embarrass the family by her attitude toward the chauffeur. Accordingly, when the party was ready to leave, they quickly bundled her into their own car.

"Ain't it pretty crowded in here?" Cora asked. "I could give you more room if I was to ride in Mr. Fairweather's auto."

"No, we want you with us," said Aunt Harriet. "You might bother Jenkins while he's driving. We want no accidents."

As the two automobiles rolled along, Jean told the entire story regarding Sonya's stolen pin.

"It was pawned by a Maggie Marsh," she concluded, "but apparently there's no one around Penfield with that name."

"I know someone with that name," spoke up Cora Appel. "In fact, she's one of my wood pile relations."

"You know someone named Maggie Marsh!" Jean exclaimed, hardly noticing the maid's amusing remark about her relative.

"She works for the Briggs family. You know, the people who have a daughter at your school. I forgot to tell you."

"Lettie!" cried Louise.

"That's the one," said Cora. "And Maggie don't like it workin' for Mrs. Briggs, neither. She says that she can't make a move without bein' watched——"

"Never mind," interposed Miss Dana dryly. "We don't care to hear idle gossip."

"Yes'm." Cora lapsed into injured silence.

"It doesn't seem possible that the Briggs's maid could have been in Penfield," Louise exclaimed.

"I had a letter from Maggie," said Applecore. "She wrote she might go to the school to help Miss Lettie pack." As the Dana girls exchanged quick glances, the maid went on, "But she's perfectly honest, Maggie is. She'd never steal nothing!"

Louise winked at Jean, saying to Applecore she was sure Maggie was honest. She made a motion with her lips, however, a motion intended only for her sister. It formed the word "Lettie."

Jean slowly moved her head in agreement.

"She did it because she dislikes Sonya for not having made friends with her," thought the girl.

"And she probably wanted the Christmas entertainment I had planned to be a failure," was Louise's silent comment.

Probably the unpleasant girl had used Maggie Marsh's name instead of her own when she had pawned the jewel. This was a double offense for which Lettie could be sent to jail. It was more than a joke and no doubt she had become afraid that she would be accused of stealing, so she had returned the pawn ticket and the money to Sonya.

Further discussion of the trouble was interrupted by Captain Dana. Sternly he reminded his nieces that they never would enjoy the trip unless the difficulty were forgotten, for the time being at least.

After that the Dana girls devoted their attention to the scenery. Cora Appel, however, was far more interested in Mr. Fairweather's car. Repeatedly she glanced through the rear window to make certain that it followed close behind them.

For an hour the Dana car climbed steadily into the mountains, each curve presenting a thrilling vista below. The road was free of snow, but on either side huge banks were piled high with it. Icicles hung from the evergreen branches, gleaming like jewels in the lowering rays of the sun.

"It's getting colder," Miss Dana remarked, drawing her fur coat snugly about her.

"I'm getting hungry," added Captain Dana. "If Tom is willing, it might be a good idea to stop at the next town for dinner."

He drew alongside the road to await the other automobile. Mr. Fairweather approved of the captain's proposal, so the party halted at a village nestled in a beautiful valley. A huge signboard directed their attention toward a restaurant bearing the name Hamlet House.

"Ah, yonder place looks inviting," declared Mr. Fairweather. "With such an illustrious name as it has, I expect an excellent dinner.''

As he led the way to the inn, Cora and Jenkins slipped away by themselves. The Danas were amused at the flirtatious glances the maid gave the chauffeur.

"I'm ready for a big porterhouse steak smothered in mushrooms," announced Tom Fairweather on the way to the dining room. "This mountain air gives one an appetite. I haven't felt so well in a long time."

"Sorry, sir," said the waitress who came to take the orders. "We don't serve steak."

"No steak! How about roast beef or veal?" asked the hearty man.

"We don't serve those either. The Hamlet House has only ham, pork, bacon, chicken and eggs in any form."

"Then they ought to call the place Ham and Omelette House!" chuckled Jean as soon as the orders had been given.

"After I've finished my meal I'll probably start crowing like a rooster or grunting like a pig!" laughed Mr. Fairweather. In a moment he became serious and said he hoped there would be no trouble at Highfort. "My lawyer advised me to come, although the final papers have not been signed. There's no question about the place being mine, but some mix-up still has to be straightened out."

The meal, although lacking a variety of

choices, was well cooked. As the party was leaving the restaurant some time later, Jenkins and Cora came slowly down the street, still arm in arm. The maid left him and sidled hopefully toward Aunt Harriet.

"If it's all right with you, Miss Dana, I'd like to ride in the other car," she whispered.

"No, Cora, I prefer that you remain with us." She spoke rather shortly, for the maid's behavior annoyed her.

"But Jenkins and I are engaged. It's right and proper a girl should ride with her future intended."

Proudly Cora displayed an imitation diamond ring which Jenkins had purchased for her at a store selling drugs, novelties and quick lunches.

"I'm goin' to have a real diamond jest as soon as Jenkins can save enough to buy it."

"Cora, you're not actually engaged!" exclaimed Miss Dana, aghast. "Why, you never met Jenkins until a day or two ago."

"It was jest a case of love at first sight," Cora said dreamily. She thumped the right side of her chest. "It hurts me here."

"Then you must have lung trouble," giggled Jean. "Your heart is nearer the left side."

Fearful lest Mr. Fairweather should hear the maid's silly talk, Miss Dana escorted her to the car. As the automobiles resumed the journey up the mountain, she delivered a stern lecture on deportment. Cora kept muttering, "Yes'm, Yes'm," in parrot fashion, but no one dared hope that she would heed advice.

Night found the party at a picturesque little inn built on the crest of Cobalt Hill. After rooms had been assigned to them, the Dana girls wandered about the lobby and for want of anything else to do examined the registry.

"Jean, look at this!" Louise exclaimed, indicating a name scrawled on the book.

"'H. V. Vitescom'!"

"What can he be doing here, I wonder?"

"Mr. Vitescom?" inquired the desk clerk who had overheard the convesation. "Oh, he left early this morning. Friend of yours?"

"An acquaintance," Jean replied.

The girls could only guess what kind of business had brought the unscrupulous man into the mountains. Probably he was on his way to blackmail someone. If they could only find him and tell the police! Jean had a special reason for disliking the fellow and she certainly could interest the authorities in her story about him.

"Did Mr. Vitescom say where he was going?" Jean inquired of the clerk.

"No, he didn't, but he seemed to be heading north."

"Was he driving? And was he alone?" asked Louise. Then by way of explaining their interest she added, "We—uh—we wonder where he is going to spend Christmas."

"That I can't tell you," replied the man behind the desk. "But he was driving with two friends. These are the ones," he indicated two scrawled signatures on the register.

"It would take a handwriting expert to figure them out," laughed Jean, but carefully noted that they were J. Thorne and P. Rinner as she turned away.

Weary from the long ride, the Dana girls went to bed early. For more than an hour the gentle snores of Cora Appel, who occupied the next room, kept them awake. Finally they fell asleep, only to be aroused by a loud cry.

"What was that?" Jean demanded, sitting up in bed.

"It sounded like Cora's voice."

Louise pulled on a bathrobe, then groped for the light switch.

"Maybe Cora is very ill," said Jean anxiously.

The Dana girls opened the door leading to the maid's bed chamber, flooding the room with light. A pillow and several blankets lay on the floor. But the bed was empty.

"Why, she isn't here!" exclaimed Louise.

"What can have happened?"

Even as Jean spoke, she noticed the open window. Darting to it, she peered downward but saw nothing. Then she looked up and was horrified by the sight which met her gaze.

Cora, ghostlike in a white nightgown, was walking along a narrow ledge at the edge of the roof! The slightest misstep would cause her to fall two stories to the ground.

"She'll slip and be killed!" added Louise fearfully. "We must do something to save her!"

CHAPTER VII

THE STORE FIRE

IN her anxiety Jean started to crawl through the open window, but Louise restrained her sister.

"Wait!" she advised. "If you climb out there you'll startle Cora. Then she'll be certain to fall."

"That's so, Louise. But what can we do? If we go for help, she'll probably tumble off while we're delaying."

"Let's talk to her naturally. I've read that one never should startle a sleepwalker."

"We can try it," Jean said dubiously. "But if it doesn't work——"

The Dana girls knew that whatever was to be done must be done quickly. Cora was walking away from them, and in another minute she would reach the end of the ledge.

"Cor-a!" Louise called softly and slowly. "Ap-ple-core!"

The maid paused, listening. Again Louise spoke the girl's name.

"Will you come here, please?" she requested in a natural voice. "Turn around very carefully."

"Is that you, Miss Louise?" the maid responded in a sleepy voice. "This street is so dark I can't see nothin'. Don't they have lights in this town?"

"You don't need a light," responded Louise soothingly. "Just turn and come straight toward me."

While the Dana girls watched with bated breath, Cora slowly revolved and started toward them. She teetered unsteadily a moment, then moved mechanically along the ledge. Jean reached out and grasped an arm, pulling her into the room.

"Lawsy me, where am I?" gasped the maid, opening her eyes and quickly closing them again. "Ain't this the street? I thought I was going down to the grocer's."

"You're in your own room in the hotel," Louise soothed her. "A moment ago you were walking in your sleep on the roof, though."

Cora looked out the window, and gave a loud, terrified scream.

"Sh!" Louise warned. "Do you want to arouse everyone in the hotel?"

With difficulty the girls quieted the maid. After getting her to bed once more they carefully locked both windows and door. The precautions were unnecessary, however, for Cora was soon fast asleep and did not stir until dawn.

After an early breakfast, the Fairweather and Dana groups again took to the road. Midafternoon found them in a small city situated some twenty miles from Highfort on Indian Mountain. As the two cars stopped at a gasoline station, Louise and Jean noticed a department store across the street.

"Aunt Harriet, I'd like to run over there and do a little shopping," Jean suggested. "I have several things I ought to buy before Christmas."

Miss Dana shared her desire to shop, so it was arranged that Mr. Fairweather and Jenkins should drive on toward the estate alone. Since they had never been there and did not know the way, they would go slowly and perhaps the others would catch up.

"I may get lost, so if you should get there first, introduce yourselves to Job Tryon and make yourselves at home," said the jolly host. "Don't worry about me."

Captain Dana looked at his friend in surprise. "Aren't you going straight to Highfort?" he asked.

"Oh yes, yes," the big man replied. "It's just that—well, nothing. Ned, would you mind coming with me a minute? I'd like a word with you."

He drew the girls' uncle aside and walked around the corner of the building. Presently the two men reappeared and Tom Fairweather stepped into his car.

"Don't spend all your money, young ladies," he joked, waving a farewell. "Old Santa Claus

Fairweather wants to give you this Christmas party, you know.''

"He's wonderful," commented Jean as the Danas crossed the street to the department store. "Oh, look at the crowd!"

Aunt Harriet and her brother decided not to brave the jostling holiday shoppers. Their nieces laughingly joined the merry group and elbowed their way through. Their attention was drawn at once to a young man who looked scornfully at a woman shopper trying to edge him away from the costume jewelry counter. The fellow held his place, and in a leisurely manner selected several unusual pieces.

"It takes some people forever to make up their minds," fidgeted the woman customer. "One would think these bracelets and things were real gems."

"They *are* copies of old museum pieces," retorted the sales clerk, annoyed. "Beautiful pieces, some of them, even if they cost only five dollars."

Smiling, the Danas passed the counter. They found it necessary to go through the toy department to reach a section where they would buy a gift for Applecore. Children milled about this young people's paradise, some with attendants, others alone.

"Oh, Louise, look at that man. He shouldn't be smoking in a crowd like this," cried Jean. "If there should be a fire——"

Hardly were the words out of her mouth than the smoker's action was noticed by someone else. A store official came hurrying down the aisle to find out who was disobeying the "No Smoking" sign.

The offender, seeing him, quickly thrust the cigarette behind his back. The next instant a paper party favor ignited. In a moment the entire counter was ablaze. Women screamed and children cried out as they were knocked down in the rush that started.

"Don't push! Don't run!" cried Jean as she lifted a child who had fallen.

The store Santa Claus leaped from his throne to put out the flames. As he bent to smother them the end of his long white beard caught fire. He was unaware of the danger but Louise sprang forward and jerked off his mask in the nick of time.

By then the crowd was thoroughly alarmed. Women, trying to save their children, fought their way to the exits. Men pushed forward roughly. Among these was the fellow who had caused the panic. He seemed to be looking for someone. Suddenly he spied the person he wanted. Over the heads of the crowd he shouted:

"We'd better get out of here, Thorne."

"Right," called the other. "Meet you at the car, Rinner."

Louise, with a child under each arm, glanced

up quickly as these words came to her ears. Thorne. Rinner. Where had she heard those names? Oh! They were Vitescom's friends! As the two men savagely leaped over a little girl who had been trampled to the floor, she said grimly to herself:

"He *would* have friends like that."

While store employees battled the flames with fire extinguishers, the two Dana girls helped guide people to the exits, their quiet, calm manner banishing the fear that had seized the crowd

By the time the toy department had been cleared, the blaze was out. As Louise and Jean were leaving, an official stopped them to express his appreciation for their work.

"We certainly are very grateful to you young ladies for your assistance," he told them.

"We're so glad the fire and panic were no worse," they smiled.

Reaching the street, the girls sought their aunt and uncle, who were waiting in the parked car. Since they had not heard about the excitement, Louise and Jean provided a modest report of their activities. The story concluded, Captain Dana glanced uneasily at his watch.

"It's getting late. Let's heave up the anchor and shove off for Highfort."

The remainder of the trip into the mountains was uneventful. But darkness descended early, and icy roads compelled Captain Dana to drive slower than he had planned.

"We should have started sooner," he grumbled. "Mr. Fairweather will wonder what has become of us."

"Uncle Ned, who is Job Tryon?" asked Louise presently.

"The man who looks after Highfort," replied the captain. "Very interesting person, I understand from Tom. He's a great naturalist and an expert on game."

"Where does he live?" asked Jean. "He does sound interesting."

"In a lodge at the edge of the estate. He is overseer of the grounds—they take in the whole mountain, you know. And there is a large game preserve on the place."

Reaching Indian Mountain, they found it to be rugged and wild. Stately evergreens lined the road leading to it. In the full moon these cast weird shadows over unbroken stretches of snow.

"I see a light ahead," announced the captain. "It may be in Tryon's lodge."

A moment later the car drew up beside an attractive log bungalow. Smoke curled lazily from the chimney of the dwelling and a radio could be heard.

"It *is* Highfort!" cried Jean gaily. She had spied a rustic marker at the side of the road.

At that moment the door of the lodge opened and a man came outside.

"Who's there?" he shouted.

"Captain Dana."

As the caretaker came quickly toward them, Louise and Jean saw that he had been followed from the building by a girl. She stepped into the beam of the car's headlights and they obtained a clear view of her face.

"My word!" exclaimed Louise in an undertone. "It's Lettie Briggs!"

Hearing her name spoken, the girl turned as if to retreat. Then, realizing that she had been recognized, she decided to face the Danas. In her mind she already was forming explanations about "the huge place with many servants" where she would be staying.

"Oh," she greeted them coldly, "what are you doing here?"

"I was just ready to ask you the same question," countered Jean. "Are you a guest at Highfort?"

"Lettie is my guest," answered the caretaker before the girl could reply. "She and her father are distant relatives of mine. I'm Job Tryon."

"You've not been invited here, have you?" Lettie demanded crossly.

"Yes, Mr. Fairweather, the new owner, is a friend of ours."

"Will you come inside and wait for him?" the caretaker invited.

"Don't tell me Tom hasn't arrived yet!" exclaimed Captain Dana, weary from the long journey.

Tryon moved closer to the car, peering quiz-zically at the occupants. He was a tall, lanky man with gnarled hands and the kind of lined face which betokened the good-natured person.

"I haven't heard from Mr. Fairweather that he is coming," the man announced. "It is unfortunate but no preparations have been made for him or any guests."

The caretaker's remarks stunned the Danas. They knew that Mr. Fairweather should have reached the estate some time ago. Aunt Harriet was annoyed at the reception as well as worried about their host.

"Perhaps he's in trouble somewhere," she exclaimed.

"Now don't start to worry, Harriet," her brother said quickly. "We noticed no place where a car had gone off the road."

Louise and Jean realized that their uncle looked troubled despite his advice.

"Then what could have become of him?" asked Aunt Harriet.

"And Jenkins," added Cora Appel in a quavering voice. "If my future intended has been hurt, I'll die of grief."

"Fairweather and Jenkins will be along soon," contributed Uncle Ned. "They may have stopped somewhere for dinner. We'll drive on to his house and wait."

"Begging your pardon, sir," the caretaker

spoke apologetically, "I haven't had any orders to admit strangers."

"We're not strangers," declared the captain, slightly irritated. "We're friends of Mr. Fairweather."

"I'm very sorry," Tryon said uneasily. "I——"

"That's right, Job," Lettie Briggs interrupted. "I shouldn't do it if I were you."

"Lettie, you *could* explain that you're well acquainted with us," said Louise, gazing steadily at the girl, "and that it would be all right for us to go on."

"Why, I know nothing of your plans. My cousin will make a big mistake if he lets you inside of Highfort."

Tossing her head impudently, Lettie retreated into the lodge, closing the door behind her.

CHAPTER VIII

A Disappearance

"Now I don't know what to do," the caretaker said, shifting uneasily from one foot to the other. "Maybe you better come inside and wait."

"After Lettie's reception, it might be better not to," spoke up Louise. "We girls go to the same school and she knows us very well, despite what she said."

"We're not close friends," added Jean quickly, "but I think I know a way to make her tell you that—" she winked at Louise.

It was not necessary to say anything more. Job Tryon smiled broadly.

"Lettie had me upset for the moment, but I ought to know she isn't always polite—not when she's out o' sorts."

"Is Mr. Briggs here?" asked Captain Dana, annoyed at the delay.

"Not at this moment. He has gone to town, but he'll be back any minute. Well, I guess it's all right for you to drive in," he said. "I'll have to open the house for Mr. Fairweather anyway, if he's coming."

Job Tryon got out his own car and led the

way. The driveway wound through an avenue
of snow-coated pines, emerging in a wide clearing at the crest of the mountain. In this stood
the mansion of Highfort, overlooking a deep
valley. In the moonlight the two-story structure had a somewhat austere appearance. Windows were dark and deep snow had drifted
against the front door.

"It'll be pretty cold inside," Tryon said, fitting a key into the lock. "But I'll get fires
started and then it'll warm up quickly."

The caretaker flooded the house with electric
light. A less cheerful sight could not have
greeted the Danas. Cora Appel shrieked.

"Ghosts! I won't stay!"

The sheet-draped furniture and the still cold
of the interior sent chills down the spines of the
visitors. Aunt Harriet was ready to leave at
once, saying this was no place for her brother
in his present state of health.

"Oh, I'm not sick," the captain protested,
"just in need of a little rest. This will do me
good."

Jean winked at Louise, then said aloud, "Applecore, how about taking off these sheets?
Maybe we'll find some Revolutionary soldiers
underneath!"

Again the maid shrieked and fled outdoors.
Here the sighing of the wind in the trees and the
flitting shadows frightened her still more. In
she came again, weeping piteously and saying

she wished her dear Jenkins would come and protect her.

"Just make yourselves at home," Job Tryon invited. "I've got to bring some kindlin' wood from the shed. I won't be gone long."

Aunt Harriet sank dejectedly into a sheet-draped chair in the living room. Her gaze wandered slowly about the place which once had served as a military post.

"This isn't the way I pictured it—" she began, but broke off as the caretaker returned with an armload of logs.

He soon had a cheerful fire blazing on the hearth. Then he went off to start a fire in the furnace while Jean and Louise uncovered the furniture. The place looked very different by the time the man returned.

"I reckon you're tired and hungry," he remarked. "I'll bring you some food from the lodge. You'll find clean bedding in the linen closet upstairs."

After the kindly man had gone, Louise and Jean explored the unusual house and then helped Cora make the beds. Soon Tryon returned with hot coffee, bread and butter, and a kettle of stew which filled the room with a tantalizing odor.

"It's not much," he apologized, "but maybe it'll tide you over until breakfast." Then he added with a smile, "I tried to get Lettie to help me, but she said she was too tired."

Jean and Louise served the simple meal at a

small table which they drew close to the fireplace. Tryon went off to look at the furnace.

"Everything seems much better to me now," Aunt Harriet declared cheerfully as Cora removed the dishes to the kitchen. "A fire is so comforting when one is tired and a little depressed."

Louise remarked that she was disappointed because the fireplaces in the house, though large and attractive, were modern. She had hoped to find the interesting old ones originally used in the fort and even discover some steps in them to the roof. But she was doomed to disappointment.

Captain Dana arose and walked to a window. He stood gazing toward the main road, a puzzled frown on his otherwise cheerful face.

"I can't understand what's detained Tom Fairweather. He should have been here long before this. I hope nothing serious has happened to him."

At this moment Tryon returned and assured the Danas everything was in working order. He hoped they would sleep well.

"Have we a telephone?" Captain Dana asked him.

"The one here is disconnected," the caretaker replied, "but I have a phone at the lodge. Do you wish to make a call, sir?"

"No, no. Thank you. I was just thinking

that Mr. Fairweather could have called you, had
he wanted to," mused Uncle Ned.

After Tryon had gone, Louise went up to her
uncle and put an arm about his shoulders. "You
are very worried, aren't you? Have you a suspicion that you haven't told us? Did Mr. Fairweather say something that upset you?"

Smiling, the sea captain patted the girl's
hand affectionately and looked into her lovely
eyes. "I see, my dear," he said, "why people in
trouble come to you to settle their problems.
Yes," he went on seriously, "Tom did confide in
me. That's why I'm concerned about him."

As he hesitated, one could have heard a pin
drop. All eyes were turned on the speaker.

"When my old friend drew me aside at that
gasoline station, he opened his wallet and
handed me several hundred dollars. 'I'm carrying too much money,' he said with a laugh.
'Since we're separating,' " the captain's voice
fell to a whisper, " 'I want you to take this with
you.' He was so insistent I finally did.

"Then I asked him what he had meant about
his not getting to Highfort ahead of us. He just
smiled and said, 'It's all right now since you
have some of the cash.' I've been wondering
this past hour whether he may have been held
up and robbed."

"You mean," asked Louise in a very low
voice, "Jenkins?"

"It's a possibility," replied her uncle, "although the chauffeur struck me as an honest young man. More than likely the two of them were waylaid."

"We'd better not let Applecore hear this," Jean advised.

Aunt Harriet was dreadfully upset over the words of her brother. The girls tried to relieve the tension by suggesting that thieves rarely do more than hold their victims for a short time, so no doubt Mr. Fairweather would communicate with them soon.

"We may as well go to bed," suggested Miss Dana at last. "Come, Ned, you are supposed to get a lot of rest and I'm extremely tired."

The captain would have preferred staying up, hoping to hear news of his friend, but he was completely exhausted after the long trip. Unwillingly, Louise and Jean followed the two up the stairs.

"I'm afraid," said the older girl as she closed the door to the bedroom the sisters had selected, "that there may be more to the story of the missing Mr. Fairweather than we suspect. Either Uncle Ned knows more than he is telling, or else his old friend Tom kept something from him."

Jean agreed, although she said hopefully that perhaps morning would bring good news. Gingerly the sisters crawled between the cold sheets, unwilling to stretch out their feet toward the bottom of the icy bed.

The wind was stronger now and howled dismally around the stone fort. Suddenly there was a blinding flash outside like lightning, but no sound followed.

"What was that?" whispered Louise.

Jumping out of bed, Jean ran to the window to peer outside. The evergreens were whipping about wildly.

"I can't see anything," she called. "But then, it's extremely dark."

"That's funny," offered Louise. "Wasn't there a light on one of those trees outside the front door? I'm sure Uncle Ned left it on."

She too hopped from the bed and tried the electric switch. The room remained in darkness.

"Oh, dear, the power is off," she exclaimed. "That flash we saw must have been the wire going down."

The girls returned to bed and in a few minutes fell asleep. It proved to be a troubled slumber and presently they were stirring restlessly.

"Jean, are you awake?" asked Louise hoarsely.

"Yes. Do you hear what I do? Someone is walking across the creaky floor in the living room," came the whispered reply.

"Maybe Mr. Fairweather is here," suggested the older girl.

The sisters sat up in bed and looked through the window. It was pitch black outside; there was no sign of automobile headlights. The two girls had the same thought at the same moment.

"Applecore!" said Louise aloud.

Quietly the sisters donned bathrobe and slippers to find out if the sleep-walking maid were prowling again. Taking a flashlight from her coat pocket, Jean led the way.

"Let's look in Cora's room first."

They tiptoed to her door, opened it and turned on the flashlight. The maid was sound asleep in her bed. Gently they closed the door.

"Listen!"

At Louise's whispered command, the girls stood still, huddled together and shivering with the cold. Distinctly they heard a creaking sound on the first floor. On tiptoe they started down the stairway.

"Who is there?" called Jean.

The question went without answer.

CHAPTER IX

STRANGE FOOTPRINTS

THE door of Captain Dana's room at the head of the stairs opened. Seeing the shadowy figures on the steps he called out:

"Stop! Who's there? What's going on here?"

He reached for the light switch but the hall remained dark. Louise came back up the steps to speak quietly to him so her aunt would not be aroused and frightened.

"Confound it, where are the lights?" the captain stormed.

"Something has happened to them," Louise told her uncle in a whisper, turning on the flashlight.

"What are you girls doing out of bed?" the man asked. "It's cold here, and I don't like you prowling around alone."

"We thought we heard someone moving about in the living room," Jean added in a hushed voice. "We thought it might be Mr. Fairweather, but when I called no one answered."

Captain Dana took the flashlight and led the way down the stairs. Reaching the living room he paused to play the beam around. "No one here now," he said.

"Jean and I were almost certain we heard someone moving about," said Louise.

"Probably the wind, or else your imagination," replied her uncle.

"Wind doesn't leave footprints!"

Dramatically the older girl pointed to a strip of carpeting illuminated by the flashlight. She stooped, touching a finger to the marks.

"Still damp! Someone walked here who had snow on his shoes!"

For a moment Captain Dana shared Louise's alarm. Then he laughed carelessly.

"Job Tryon must have been in. He may have come to bring more wood."

"There's none on the hearth."

"I'll look around the house just to satisfy you," chuckled the captain. "But I am sure it was the caretaker who was here."

"Then why didn't he answer me when I called?" asked Jean.

Accompanied by the two girls, Uncle Ned made the round of rooms, looking into closets and under furniture. No intruder was discovered and nothing seemed to have been touched. Captain Dana, though mystified, was not alarmed and insisted they all return to bed. Jean and Louise preferred to dress, however, for it was nearly dawn and they could not fall asleep again.

"It's a funny thing about these footprints," Jean remarked as she re-examined the marks on the rug by daylight. "They lead across the room to the wall opposite the fireplace."

"The marks lead in only one direction," said Louise.

"Why, so they do!" cried Jean. "I didn't notice that."

"Then how did the intruder get out of the house?"

"He must have backed out, using his own shoe tracks," chuckled Jean.

Before she could say more, a light tap sounded on the front door. Then a key was inserted in the lock and Job Tryon walked in.

"Mornin'," he said cheerfully. "Just thought I'd run over and get your fires started. Sleep well last night?"

Louise chose her words carefully. "Not very well," she answered. "The wind disturbed us and cut off the lights. Then we heard you come in during the early morning hours, and that naturally awakened us."

The caretaker dropped his wood on the hearth with a loud clatter, as if he were greatly surprised.

"You didn't hear me. No, sir!" he said emphatically.

The Dana girls said no more until the man had gone, for they were sure he was telling the truth. After the door had closed behind him they studied the stains on the carpet with new interest.

"I have a feeling that the mysterious caller last night was no ordinary burglar," Jean commented. "Do you suppose his coming had anything to do with Mr. Fairweather?"

Louise did not reply at once. She was staring ahead of her. "Maybe the intruder was after something hidden in the wall," she said at last.

"What makes you think so?"

"The footprints lead to the north wall and stop."

"Suggesting that the person might have gone through a secret panel or door?"

"That's what I was thinking, Jean. Don't forget this house was constructed from an old fort. There may be a lot of hidden and mysterious entrances and exits in this place."

Greatly impressed by her sister's theory, Jean began tapping on the wall with her knuckles.

"It sounds solid as a rock," she reported. "Guess you'll have to get a new idea, Louise."

"That makes the mystery all the more intriguing," the older girl rejoined. "I'm so glad we were invited to Highfort."

Jean's pounding had awakened Miss Dana, and soon the entire household was astir. Tryon brought breakfast supplies from his own shelves. Cora tried to prepare a meal, but after the clumsy girl had dropped two eggs on the kitchen floor, Miss Dana took over the task.

"I dunno what's wrong with me," the maid moaned, her hands shaking. "I keep thinkin' about Jenkins. I kin see him buried in a snow-drift with the car on top an'——"

"Cora!" her mistress reproved. "Try not to express such thoughts. We're all worried. Don't make it worse."

The morning wore on slowly with no word received from Mr. Fairweather or his chauffeur. Apprehension increased, and the Danas debated what they should do.

"We can't stay here without supplies," said Miss Dana. "Perhaps we had better go back to Oak Falls."

At this her brother and nieces protested. They wanted to stay, a little longer at least, to try to find out what they could of a possible mishap to the owner of Highfort and they had not forgotten the unexplained footprints in the living room.

"Ned, you came for a rest," protested his sister, "but instead you are worrying."

"Well, all right, Harriet," the captain smiled. "I'll put the girls in charge of the mystery. We'll stay a little longer and I can rest up for the trip back."

"Jean and I could drive to the nearest town and buy whatever we need," Louise offered. "While there we might inquire if anyone saw Mr. Fairweather."

In the end it was decided that the girls should

make the trip. They dressed warmly, for the day was cold despite a bright sun. As their car approached Tryon's lodge, Louise caught a glimpse of Lettie Briggs.

The girl was dressed in a scarlet hunting coat with a bright red cap of matching color. Over her shoulder, in awkward fashion, she carried a shotgun. At a wink from Jean, Louise stopped the car.

"Hello, Lettie," she called. "My goodness, what are you doing with that gun?"

"I am out after a few rabbits," the girl replied haughtily. "Possibly a bear or so."

"Did Mr. Tryon give you permission to carry a gun?" Louise inquired in disapproval.

Lettie's slight hesitation made it evident that she had taken the weapon without consulting her cousin.

"What's it to you?" she asked coldly.

"I was only thinking of your safety, Lettie."

"And the safety of the sheriff," Jean added mischievously.

"What sheriff?"

"Why, didn't you know, Lettie? Mr. Closson is scouting the highways for a jewel thief. He's after the one who pawned a diamond pin and used another person's name."

A frightened expression came into Lettie's eyes.

"Is—is Mr. Closson near here now?"

"He might be," said Jean gravely. "Just

be careful if he should pop out of the woods suddenly.''

''You're just being smart,'' Lettie retorted, recovering her poise. ''Anyway, why should I be afraid of the sheriff?''

''Why, indeed?'' laughed Jean meaningly.

The Danas might have pursued the subject but decided that at the moment their errands were more important. In the town of Ashton they bought supplies, then started their inquiry regarding the Fairweather car. None of the storekeepers had observed the chauffeur-driven automobile. At the near-by office of the state troopers they learned that no motor accident on the roads had been reported.

''At least no news should be good news,'' Louise remarked as the girls left the place and walked slowly to their parked sedan. ''But I'm still uneasy about the idea of a hold-up.''

So concerned were the girls that as they entered their car they barely glanced toward a man who sat in a parked automobile. He saw them, however, and immediately started his motor.

Not until his car was putting on speed did Louise and Jean notice him. The driver was a thin dark man with a black mustache. Although he looked vaguely familiar, they could not recall where they had seen him before.

The car sped away. Suddenly Jean cried out and told her sister to follow him.

''That man is Vitescom!''

"But Vitescom has no mustache!"

"You mean he had none when we last met him. He's wearing a false one as a disguise!"

"But why, Jean?"

"That's what I want to know," returned her sister soberly. "Come on, Louise, let's find out where that purse snatcher and blackmailer is staying. I have a little score to settle with him!"

Backing the car from the parking space, Louise quickly drove after the Vitescom automobile. It was out of sight now and when they came to a crossroads they did not know which way to turn. Deciding it would be a waste of time to follow further, they abandoned the search.

"I'd like to know what he's up to around here," said Louise. "No good, I'm sure of that."

"Especially since he has on a disguise," agreed Jean. "Do you suppose those two friends of his are in this vicinity too?"

"I don't know. But there's one thing that I just thought of. Vitescom was very interested in jewels. His friend was buying a lot of imitation stuff. At the time it seemed to me to be a lot of costume jewelry for one man to buy, even for Christmas gifts."

"I doubt that there's any connection," replied her sister, "and yet, a good detective never misses the slightest clue," she laughed. "So maybe the great Dana sleuths will uncover a robbery never before thought of by the mind of Man.''

This light mood did not last long, for the two girls could not entirely rid themselves of an uneasy feeling about Vitescom. Arriving at the estate, Louise called attention to fresh tire tracks on the snowy road.

"A car has been here since we left, Jean! That means probably Mr. Fairweather has arrived. What a relief!''

Disappointment awaited the girls at the fortress home. There they learned that the newcomers were Mrs. Huguson Lancaster Plimpton and her maid Marybelle. The information was imparted by Cora, who met the girls at the kitchen door.

"Miss Dana's jest as upset as she can be," Applecore revealed in a whisper. "The fat lady busts right in here claimin' she owns this place.''

CHAPTER X

A Robbery

The sisters looked at each other horrified. Someone else claiming the estate! So Mr. Fairweather did not own it after all! This might explain his absence and yet what a predicament in which to put the Danas.

"It's an awful mess," said Applecore. "And you should see Miss Daisy. She's the biggest woman I ever laid eyes on."

"Miss Daisy?" Jean inquired, puzzled. "How many people are there?"

"Oh, there's just two. The grand lady and her maid. The lady is the fat one. Her name is Mrs. Huguson Lancaster Plimpton, only Marybelle calls her Miss Daisy. That's on account of her ma havin' worked for the Plimpton family for so many years. She's a snip too, Marybelle is! Right off she says to me——"

"You say Mrs. Plimpton claims she owns this place?" Louise interrupted hastily.

"That's her story. Her husband owned Highfort but he died. She's a widow now. Oh, she's been stormin' all over the place, sayin' she never sold it to Mr. Fairweather. We all got to leave right away."

86

"What does Uncle Ned say?" questioned Jean anxiously. "He must be upset by this new turn of events."

"He don't have a chance to get a word in edgewise. She keeps shoutin' like she thought we all was deaf."

Mrs. Plimpton's voice plainly could be heard from the main room of the house.

"You are intruders here!" she said shrilly. "Intruders! Highfort has not been sold to anyone. You are to leave at once. Do I make myself clear?"

"Mrs. Plimpton," rejoined Captain Dana, "if you will try to calm yourself we'll talk this over sensibly. Give me a chance to look into the facts in the case."

"Highfort belongs to me! There's nothing more to be said. Kindly leave the premises at once. All of you!"

Uncle Ned's jaw stiffened. "Mrs. Plimpton, we are not leaving," he said firmly. "We are staying right here."

"You dare defy me? I'll call the sheriff— I'll have you arrested!"

"I'll welcome an investigation of our presence here. We are guests of Mr. Fairweather, remember that, please."

"I never heard of him," cried the woman, her face very red.

"Possibly not, but he purchased Highfort from the men taking care of your late husband's

estate. The property was sold with all its fur-
nishings.''

"I don't believe it," Mrs. Plimpton cried angrily. "The sale wouldn't be good without my
signature."

"Aren't you forgetting that you have a le-
gally appointed attorney to sign such things?"
Captain Dana asked.

Mr. Fairweather had told him that the widow's financial affairs had been taken from her
hands and turned over to a reliable guardian.

"Oh! Oh! You cruel, unkind man!" Mrs.
Plimpton accused. Clapping a hand to the re-
gion of her heart, she staggered backward. "My
smelling salts, Marybelle! I feel faint!"

The maid ran to her mistress's side, offering
her a supporting arm. "You've excited Miss
Daisy," she cried, glaring at Captain Dana.

"My smelling salts!" Mrs. Plimpton called
weakly. "Quick!"

"Oh, Miss Daisy, they're still packed in the
suitcase."

"Then I shall faint. I feel myself slipping
away—slipping——"

It was plain to everyone except the maid that
Mrs. Plimpton was acting a part. From the
doorway Louise and Jean had witnessed the entire scene.

"The water pitcher," said the latter impishly.
"Shall we dump the contents on her?"

The girl might have carried through her

threat had not the caretaker appeared. At once Mrs. Plimpton sat up and appealed to him.

"Oh you," she ordered, "drive these dreadful people out of here. They're—they're just bar-berarians!" Louise and Jean could hardly suppress smiles at the mispronunciation of the word "barbarian."

Poor Job was at a loss what to do, for he and his former mistress never had met and he had understood she was a queer person. He had heard her husband say many times that the first thing to be done after his death was to offer Highfort for sale. On the other hand, the caretaker did not know Fairweather or the Danas. Finally the naturalist's keen sense of reading character decided the issue.

"Suppose you go upstairs and rest, Mrs. Plimpton," he advised kindly, "and I'll see what I can do."

With a glare at the Danas the woman stormed up the steps, Marybelle behind her. Fortunately her bedroom had not been used, but remarks about dust and cold reached the ears of those below.

"Captain Dana," said Tryon uneasily, "I don't know what to do. I'm in a bad spot. I wish we'd hear something from Mr. Fairweather. That would settle matters."

"I wish so too," replied Uncle Ned. "We had planned to stay one more day. How about leaving it that way?"

The caretaker smiled broadly. "I don't want to be left here alone with Mrs. Plimpton, so you'll do me a favor that way by staying. She is—well, that is—she was pretty hard to get along with and so her husband didn't ever let her come up here. I'm kind of afraid of what she might do to the place if she gets mad."

"We must remain until Mr. Fairweather comes or she goes," said Captain Dana with determination. "Otherwise there will be no one to protect his interests."

Cora Appel appeared in the doorway, listening with mouth agape. She had just come downstairs.

"Oh, we ought to stay," she contributed. "I just heard Miss Daisy tell Marybelle to start packin' up the good china."

"Let us know if that happens," said Aunt Harriet, worried. "Now please go to the kitchen and start luncheon. Jean and Louise have brought supplies."

"I ain't cookin' no food for that Miss Daisy, or Marybelle either," Cora muttered in a sullen voice as she left the room.

"Cora is quite hopeless today," sighed Miss Dana. "The poor girl fears now that maybe Jenkins has failed to come here because he intends to jilt her!"

"The explanation isn't that simple, I'm afraid," said Captain Ned. "No news from town, Jean?"

"We inquired everywhere, Uncle Ned. Mr. Fairweather's car hasn't been seen nor heard of."

Before the girls could mention Mr. Vitescom, a loud crash drew them to the kitchen.

"Applecore, what have you done now?" Jean asked wearily.

The flustered maid had upset a pan of peas from the stove. As she tried to scoop the peas from the floor, she knocked two dishes from a table and broke them.

"If Miss Dana finds out about this she'll send me back to Oak Falls," the girl wailed. "Then I'll maybe never get my real diamond ring."

"I thought you had decided Jenkins changed his mind," said Jean.

"But I changed mine again," replied Applecore. "I had a kind of vision and saw a real diamond on my finger!"

The Dana girls helped Cora sweep the floor. Afterwards they set the dining room table and helped cook the meal, for the absent-minded maid seemed incapable of work.

"Now do be careful when you serve," Louise cautioned her when everything was ready.

Upon being called to luncheon, Mrs. Plimpton appeared in a long velvet gown suitable only for formal occasions.

"I know I'll be unable to eat a bite," she announced aloofly. "My nervous system is very breakable."

Captain Dana winked at his nieces as he slid the woman's chair into place. The food was excellent, but the widow offered many complaints. Notwithstanding her professed lack of appetite, she ate more than anyone else.

The Danas were annoyed one minute and amused the next at her funny use of words. In the midst of dessert, Marybelle suddenly ran into the dining room.

"Miss Daisy!" she cried. "Something dreadful has happened."

"Why, Marybelle, what is wrong?"

"Your jewels! They've been stolen from the special suitcase!"

"My beautiful diamond ring?"

"Everything's gone, Miss Daisy. The jewels have been taken since we came to Highfort!" the maid announced breathlessly.

Mrs. Plimpton arose from her chair slowly. Her gaze wandered accusingly from one to another of the Dana family.

"Someone in this room is responsible for my loss!" she exclaimed. "I've been robbed by one of you!"

"The jewels may have been misplaced—" Captain Dana began, only to be cut short.

"I've been robbed! Where is the phone? I'm going to call the sheriff."

To the Danas' consternation the heavy-set woman lumbered across the room to the telephone desk. Taking the receiver from its hook she tried for many minutes to summon an operator.

"This wire is dead!" she cried. "You've cut the line to prevent me from calling!"

"It was disconnected some time ago by the company," said Uncle Ned coldly.

Mrs. Plimpton slammed the receiver on the hook, just as Cora appeared with a plate of cookies.

"If you ask me," said Marybelle, pointing at the Dana maid, "she's the one who is the thief. She was talking all morning about getting a diamond ring."

At this accusation Applecore dropped the plate of cookies to the floor and sagged against the wall. "I never stole nothin' in my life," she moaned.

The widow listened for a moment, then took charge again. "As soon as I can get the sheriff here I'll have him question everyone in the house. Come upstairs, Marybelle."

Uncle Ned was so convinced the story of the robbery was a hoax that he remained in the dining room, but his nieces dashed off, looking into closets and other places where a thief might be hiding. When they reached Mrs. Plimpton's quarters, the woman interrupted their work by another tirade.

Upon being questioned closely, the widow said that besides the diamond ring the only valuable piece missing was a bracelet. The rest of the trinkets were just inexpensive costume jewelry.

The sisters continued their search for clues, this time going outdoors. To their delight they found footprints which were fresh and undisturbed. They led from the front door around one side of the fortress home and into the woods.

"These are about the same size as those prints we found on the rug last night!" Louise observed excitedly.

Running, the girls followed the impressions of a man's boots. They led to a little-used road and ended where there were auto tracks.

"So the thief used a car," surmised Jean, as they turned back.

Returning to the mansion, the sisters were startled to hear the loud report of a gun. Simultaneously there came the sound of splintering glass and a shrill scream.

"Gunfire," said Louise tersely, running to the door. "Someone fired through one of the windows!"

CHAPTER XI

SHATTERED GLASS

ANXIOUSLY the Dana girls went from room to room. Hearing sobs from within a hall closet, Jean jerked open the door. Out staggered Cora, her eyes dilated with terror.

"What has happened?" Jean demanded. "Where is everyone? Who fired the shot?"

At first the maid was too frightened to speak. She shook as if from a chill and her teeth chattered.

"S-somebody killed Mrs. P-Plimpton. Shot at her right through the window and he's goin' to git us all, one by one. Oh me, why'd I ever come to this wicked place?"

With all speed the girls raced to the widow's room. The woman lay on the bed groaning, while her maid, Aunt Harriet and Captain Dana hovered anxiously beside her.

"I tell you I've been shot," Mrs. Plimpton moaned. "The bullet came right through the window. It must have struck me in the chest."

"A shot was fired, but fortunately, it didn't strike you, Mrs. Plimpton," Miss Dana said, trying to soothe her. "There's no wound."

While she and Marybelle spoke comfortingly

to the hysterical woman, Jean, Louise and their uncle searched for evidence of the bullet. Opposite the shattered window they found a lead bullet buried in the wood paneling.

Hoping to learn who had discharged the weapon, the sisters hurried outdoors. No one was in sight, but Louise discovered freshly made tracks in the snow. They had been made by someone running.

Quickly the girls followed the trail. To their amazement the telltale markings led them to the door of Tryon's bungalow!

"Do you suppose Lettie could have fired the shot?" asked Jean in an undertone. "But why?"

She rapped on the door. Not a sound could be heard inside and no one answered the knock.

"If she's hiding," Louise said grimly, "I'll get her out! Why, she might have killed someone!"

Pounding again, she called in a loud voice that unless the door were opened she would summon the sheriff. The threat worked like magic. In another moment Lettie, her hair disheveled, her face pale, peered out at the Danas.

"You didn't expect us to find out so soon what's been going on, did you?" Louise asked, looking straight at Lettie.

"What do you want here?"

"I think you know," Jean said soberly. "What have you done with your hunting equipment?"

"Tell me—has—has anyone been hurt?" the Briggs girl asked tremulously.

"Then it *was* you who fired the shot through the window?" Louise demanded.

Lettie backed away from her accusers. "Don't have me arrested," she quavered. "I didn't mean to do it. I—I was aiming at a rabbit."

"Inside the house?" Jean caught her up.

"I—I closed my eyes when I pulled the trigger. Then I heard glass breaking and knew I'd hit a window pane. I was so scared I ran. Has—has anyone been killed?"

"No," Louise said, taking pity upon the girl. "Mrs. Plimpton was badly frightened but fortunately the bullet missed her."

"Oh, I'm so thankful. So thankful."

Lettie's mental suffering had been intense, and the Dana girls felt that she had been punished sufficiently. Their plan of speaking about Maggie Marsh and the diamond pin the next time they saw her was not carried through. They would wait. Instead, Jean carelessly turned the conversation to the subject of shoes and learned that Tryon wore a very large size.

"Whatever made you talk about that?" asked Louise on the way back to the mansion.

"I am planning to do a little work on prints this afternoon. Foot and finger," laughed her sister.

For some time the girls worked on the case but found nothing to aid them in identifying the thief from his marks in the snow.

"I'm glad to eliminate Tryon, for I like him," said Louise. "It certainly wasn't he who tracked the carpet, or made the marks outdoors, for his shoe size is much too large."

The Dana family held a council of war late in the afternoon. Should they pack their bags or should they stay, was the question. Aunt Harriet wanted to go; she thought the place was spooky and the work too hard. Her brother still felt that he should protect his friend Fairweather's interests against the unreliable Mrs. Plimpton. Louise and Jean were loath to leave the mystery unsolved.

"We certainly couldn't do anything about the jewel thief in Oak Falls," the younger girl pointed out in wheedling tones.

"Mr. Fairweather disappeared near here and we ought to start a search for him from this point," argued Louise.

Aunt Harriet threw up her hands and laughed. "It's no use," she said. "All right, then. We'll stay. But I'd like a little Christmas spirit put into this vacation. How about a tree and——"

The girls hugged her and promised to carry out her wishes. Uncle Ned was given the task of cutting down an evergreen. His sister and Cora went to look for some pine boughs and cones to decorate the house. Louise and Jean drove to the village to buy ornaments.

"And as soon as we do that, let's work on the mystery a little more," said Louise enthusiastically as they reached Ashton.

At Highfort her uncle had drawn her aside and requested her to make an important telephone call while in the village. Assigning Jean the task of selecting tree lights and ornaments, Louise went to the nearest telephone booth.

Her first number was the city apartment where Mr. Fairweather spent much of his time. The telephone was answered by a housekeeper who said at once that she had not heard from her employer in more than a week.

Upon her own initiative Louise then called Starhurst School and talked with Mrs. Crandall. The headmistress assured her that Mr. Fairweather had left no message for the Danas at the institution.

As a last resort, Louise telephoned to Oak Falls to a neighbor who had promised to look after the Danas' mail during their absence. The woman could provide no news regarding the missing man.

"So that's that," Louise said to Jean as she rejoined her sister. "The mystery remains as deep as ever."

"What's our next move?"

"Uncle Ned told me that if all else failed we should report the disappearance to the state troopers."

"Before we do that, let's go into a few stores here and ask if anyone has been trying to sell jewelry lately," suggested Jean.

Not a clue did they get, though they received strange looks from the busy shopkeepers. At last they turned their steps toward the office of the state police, where a lone trooper was in attendance. His smile of greeting turned to one of concern as the Danas unfolded the adventures in connection with Highfort.

"We'll get to work on these matters at once," promised the officer. "I'll send a couple of men up to your place to look for footprints of the thief and start some phoning myself in regard to this Mr. Fairweather."

"Perhaps we can save you some trouble," said Louise, producing a drawing of the mysterious prints left on the carpet and in the snow.

"My goodness," laughed the trooper, "this is the first time two young ladies ever did part of my work for me. This is very good—very good, indeed."

The sisters blushed and took their leave. "Our phone isn't working, but the one at Tryon's bungalow is," Louise said in parting. "If we can be of any help, please let us know."

As the girls drew up to the front door of the mansion at Highfort a little later they met the other returning members of the family and Cora. Uncle Ned and the maid were carrying a pine tree. Aunt Harriet was laden down with forest greens.

"Where do you want the Christmas tree put?" asked Uncle Ned.

"You might set it at the end of the trail—the trail of the strange footprints," giggled Jean. "This tree marks the spot where the mystery ended."

This was done and the captain declared only an earthquake could knock over the beautiful evergreen. The group became jolly, trying to forget the sinister atmosphere that hung over the place. The task of decorating the Christmas tree was one Louise and Jean thoroughly enjoyed. They carefully hung on the ornaments and lights and Cora helped by attaching strings of tinsel.

"It's jest as purty a tree as we ever had in Oak Falls," the maid declared when the work was finished. "But it don't look right without any presents."

"The tree shall have presents," laughed Jean.

Nearly all the gifts which had been purchased had cost less then fifty cents and were intended to provoke merriment.

"Now here is something," said Jean to her sister. She held up a small black patent leather purse. "Do we dare give it to Mrs. Plimpton?"

The pocketbook was a trick gadget which

would send off an electrical shock when opened. Originally the girls had bought it intending to play a joke on Cora.

"Say, Jean, I have a better idea! That shiny patent leather should leave a plain fingerprint!"

"It does. What's your idea, Louise?"

"Let's hang it on the tree unwrapped. Then if our mysterious visitor should come here he may try to steal it with disastrous results."

"I think it would be better to drop it into a chair close by," replied Jean. "That way, the prowler might assume it contained money."

The girls made a point of being with Captain Dana when he locked the doors for the night. Not one was overlooked.

"If any one should try to get in here tonight, we'll catch the scamp," said the captain confidently.

As Louise kissed her uncle good night, she asked him if he had Mr. Fairweather's money put away safely.

"My dear, it's with me night and day. Any fellow trying to get it would have to get me first!" the man chuckled.

This was not a very comforting thought, and the girl lay awake a long time worrying about it. At last she fell asleep, and it was dawn when Jean nudged her.

"Wake up, Louise."

"Did you hear something?" her sister asked drowsily.

"I don't know. There's no noise now, but I woke up out of a sound sleep."

"Let's see if the pocketbook has been touched."

Rolling out of bed, the girls tiptoed down the half dark stairway to the living room. Jean raised a blind which admitted the early morning light.

"Look, Louise!" she cried. "Someone *has* been here!"

The beautiful Christmas tree, many of its ornaments broken, lay on the floor!

CHAPTER XII

Mysterious Happenings

Upon seeing the overturned tree, Louise and Jean were certain that the mysterious intruder had paid Highfort another call during the night. But why had he knocked over the tree and how had he entered the place?

"There's no one here now," declared Louise in a whisper. "I wonder if the fellow left any footprints?"

She dropped on hands and knees to inspect the carpet, but could find no damp spots or mud tracks.

"Possibly he left fingerprints on the pocketbook!" exclaimed Jean hopefully.

Darting to the chair by the fireplace, she snatched up the purse. Instantly she squealed with pain and dropped it again.

"That was smart, I must say!" chuckled Louise. "What a memory you have, dear sister."

"I forgot about it giving off a shock. Anyway, I don't believe the purse was touched during the night," she added, examining it.

Just then Captain Dana appeared. "What's going on here?" he asked in a deep voice.

"Oh, Uncle Ned, just see our lovely Christmas tree," wailed Jean. "It was upset during the night. Half the ornaments are ruined."

"Queer." The captain padded across the room in slipper feet to inspect the metal holder. "I flattered myself I did a particularly good job of setting it up."

Louise began to collect broken pieces of glass from the carpet.

"At first we were sure someone had bumped into the tree," she said quietly, "but there are no footprints."

"And the doors and windows are locked," added Jean after testing them. "I guess the tree must have tumbled by itself."

"I'm so sure I set it securely in place," objected Uncle Ned, "that I could almost believe some spook did the mischief."

"That same spook didn't get Mr. Fairweather's wallet by any chance, did he?" Jean asked.

The sea captain tapped his pajama pocket significantly. "I—" Suddenly a queer expression came over his face. "It's—it's gone!"

For several seconds no one spoke. The big man turned deathly pale and slumped into a chair. Louise was the first to speak, and her words were practical.

"When did you last see the money?" she asked.

"As I got into bed, I put it into my pocket."

Quickly the two girls hurried up the stairs, searching each step of the way for the missing wallet. Reaching their uncle's room they looked on the floor, in the bed and among his clothes without success. By this time the captain had reached the second floor. Having recovered from his astonishment, he declared nobody could have taken the money without his knowing it.

"There's just one more place to look," said Jean hopefully, going again to the bed.

This time she pulled off all the covers and felt in the space between the mattress and the footboard. Suddenly her face lighted up and she produced the lost wallet. The money was intact.

"You must have had a bad dream and hid it there, Uncle Ned," laughed his niece.

The captain's face took on a serious look. "That's funny. Now that you mention it, I remember having a nightmare; at least it seemed like one. Someone was trying to get the money but I hid it. The dream seemed very real."

The sisters looked at each other significantly. Maybe it had *not* been all a dream. More than likely some thief had been frustrated in an attempt to steal the wallet. With sober thoughts the two girls went to their room to dress.

Following breakfast, Captain Dana righted the Christmas tree and changed the location of it to make it more secure than before. The branches had not been damaged, but so many

ornaments were broken that the girls decided to
drive to town for additional ones.

"While there you may as well buy a turkey,"
Miss Dana suggested. "And all the things to go
with it."

Learning that Louise and Jean were driving
to the village, Mrs. Plimpton presented them
with a long list of articles which she wished for
herself. Although she heard plans being made
for the holiday feast, she did not offer to con-
tribute either money or labor.

"The least she could do would be to have
Marybelle help Applecore in the kitchen," Jean
remarked as the girls motored along the snowy
country road. "All she does is eat and com-
plain!"

"I suppose she feels that everything at Highfort belongs to her. Oh dear, I wish we would
hear something from or about genial Mr. Fairweather."

Reaching Ashton, the girls did the marketing,
then wearily started on the widow's list. Looking up from a counter, they saw Lettie Briggs
standing near by.

"Oh, hello," she greeted them with unusual
cordiality. "All ready for Christmas?"

With an attempt at carelessness, the girl
flipped open her coat, exposing a pin set with
red and white stones. Louise and Jean could
not fail to notice it, but they made no comment.

"See my Christmas present," Lettie said

proudly. "Isn't the pin a beauty? And it was given to me by a man—a very handsome man, I might add."

The Dana girls politely examined the ornament but had little to say. They were satisfied that only a trifling sum had been paid for it.

"You never could guess who gave it to me," Lettie went on mysteriously. "The pin is a family heirloom."

"Indeed?" Louise hid a smile.

"I received it as a reward. You see, I've been gathering important information for this gentleman."

"Oh, you were acting as a confidential investigator?" Jean asked, winking at her sister.

"That's right. He gave me the gift because he valued my services so highly."

"By chance the man isn't Mr. Vitescom?" questioned Louise.

"Oh, no. His name is Trout—Holweg Trout. He's very handsome."

The name meant nothing to Louise or Jean. They were curious as to the nature of the information imparted by Lettie but she gave them no hint.

"Christmas here on Indian Mountain is going to be so dreary," she said, quickly changing the subject. "You know, it's the first time I've ever spent the holidays away from my mother. She had to go see her sister who is ill in California."

Lettie presented such a long, doleful face that

the Dana girls could not fail to feel sorry for her.

"It's no fun staying at my cousin's," she went on. "He doesn't like me and he doesn't like Christmas. We're not even having a tree."

"Oh, that's a pity," Louise replied with sincerity. Impulsively she added, "Why not come up to the house tonight? We're all planning upon hanging stockings and having Christmas Eve festivities."

"I'll be glad to come."

Lettie spoke with alacrity and the smile which lighted her face had a slight suggestion of triumph. Too late it occurred to Louise that she might have made a mistake in extending the invitation. Was it not possible that the Briggs girl had a special reason for wishing to visit the mansion of Highfort?

"I'll see you tonight," Lettie said, and swung off down the street.

"I wish you hadn't invited her," Jean remarked a moment later. "I have a feeling of suspicion she deliberately set a trap for us."

"I'm afraid of it too," Louise agreed. "Anyway, it's done now and we can't retreat. But we'll keep our eyes open."

Finishing their shopping, the girls motored back to the estate. As they entered a side door of the fortress home, Mrs. Plimpton's shrill voice broke upon their ears.

"Of all the highhanded affronts this is positively the worst," she stormed. "This estate is mine, and no one can drive me away from it! I've been treated ignobly, igdominionously—and in my own home!"

"Mrs. Plimpton will choke sometime on one of her big words," chuckled Jean. "I guess she must mean ignominiously."

Another voice answered the excited woman, a soft cool voice which struck the Dana girls as strangely familiar. The words were spoken with a slight accent.

"My brother and I do not wish to drive you away. But you must understand—Highfort is ours."

"That voice—" murmured Jean. "It can't be——"

"Sonya!" completed Louise impressively. "I'm sure of it! But what can she be doing here?"

CHAPTER XIII

Two Prisoners

Louise and Jean hurried to the main hall. At a glance they saw that the girl who had dared defy Mrs. Plimpton was Sonya Olavu. Behind her stood a young man of military bearing whom they took to be her brother.

"Oh!" Mrs. Plimpton whirled to face Louise and Jean. "I didn't hear you girls come in. Tell these two young upstarts that they must leave Highfort at once!"

Ignoring the excited woman, the Dana sisters smiled reassuringly at Sonya.

"Louise! Jean!" she cried, her face brightening. "How you came to be here I do not know! But how glad I am to see you! Everything is in what you call a tangle."

As Sonya ran to clasp the Dana girls' hands in a warm greeting, Mrs. Plimpton stared from one to another. Gradually it dawned upon her that they were old friends.

"You are all in this together!" she gasped. "It is a scheme to rob me of Highfort! Oh, oh, I feel faint. Marybelle! My smelling salts!"

"What does she mean?" Sonya asked in perplexity as the woman retreated to her room. "Why is she here in this house? I do not understand. She is a stranger to me. Surely my brother and I are the owners of Highfort! We have papers——"

"It's a long story," sighed Louise. "As you said yourself, everything is in what you call a tangle. You don't even know why we're here."

"Sonya," spoke the young man, "you have not yet presented me to your friends."

"Oh, a thousand pardons! I am so excited, I forget you have not met," she cried, embarrassed and flustered.

Upon being introduced, Tranley Olavu soberly bowed to Louise and Jean. He resembled Sonya slightly, and had friendly, expressive eyes like hers.

"My sister has told me about you," he said, speaking slowly. "You have been very kind to her and I am grateful."

The Dana girls were very happy to be reunited with their school friend, although mystified by her sudden appearance at Highfort. After Uncle Ned and Aunt Harriet had met the newcomers, Tranley Olavu offered a complete explanation of their presence on Indian Mountain.

"For many years Highfort has belonged to the Olavu family. Originally this estate was the property of my father's brother, but later it was deeded to Sonya and me. Someone—a dishonest person—learned that we were in Europe and that the property remained unoccupied.

Fake deeds were written, and the place was sold to a man named Plimpton.''

"Why, Mrs. Plimpton is the one who caused such a scene only a moment ago,'' contributed Jean. "Didn't you know her name?''

"She didn't take time to tell us,'' Tranley smiled meaningly.

"Have you a deed to show that you own Highfort?'' inquired Captain Dana gravely.

"Yes, sir, we have. And I have checked to see that it is properly recorded.''

"Then what about Mr. Fairweather?'' asked Aunt Harriet. "He thought he bought the property from Mrs. Plimpton's attorney.''

The situation had become slightly ridiculous with the ownership of Highfort more in doubt than ever. While the Dana girls did not question the sincerity of Sonya and her brother, Uncle Ned was apt to be cautious and not ready to accept Tranley's explanation.

"If only Mr. Fairweather were here we could sift this matter through,'' sighed Aunt Harriet.

Louise spoke of the Danas' decision to remain for the holidays and Sonya was delighted. Both she and her brother expressed concern over the disappearance of Mr. Fairweather and offered to do anything they could to help find him.

Meanwhile, in a spot not far distant, a strange scene was being enacted. Before burning logs in a fireplace two men sat talking.

"This is good coffee," said the heavier of the two companions, "and good hamburgers, too. You're quite a cook, Pete."

"Yeh," responded the one complimented, "I don't mind doing a little but I don't aim to keep it up, an' I hate to clean the mess in the kitchen after every meal."

The speaker looked moodily into the blazing wood. "How about rousing the younger guy in the den and puttin' him to work?"

"Do you think we can, after givin' 'em the sleeping powder?" pondered the second fellow. "Brains might get sore," he concluded gloomily, sipping his drink.

"I don't think he'll pop in right away. I'll bet some of his plans have gone haywire already. He looks worried to me."

"He certainly is secretive about the layout. Three days now and he hasn't told us hardly anything. If I don't get some real money for this job, there's goin' to be trouble," growled Pete.

"Same here, Jack. The older prisoner looks like money to me. The young feller is his chauffeur, so of course there's a bank account somewhere to pay for him and that swell car."

"Well, this ain't cleanin' the kitchen," muttered Pete, rising and slowly stacking the dishes. "Shall we risk loosening Jenkins an' make him do it?"

"Sure."

The two men cautiously unlocked a small door at the end of the living room. They stepped inside to a dark den. Windowless walls lined with deep built-in bookcases made the room an ideal hide-out for the two guarded inmates. Not one sound could penetrate to the outside world. Two sofas held the bound figures in the silent gloom.

Pete and Jack shook the uniformed chauffeur. The sleeper blinked and stretched himself awake. "Oh, you again," he said weakly, rubbing a cold hand across his forehead. "Who are you anyway?" he asked, staring at the two men bending over him.

"We're not sayin'," growled Jack. "You're not to talk, just follow orders!"

"Is Mr. Fairweather still here?" continued Jenkins, looking around the dark room.

Seeing the silent figure on the other couch he moved toward his employer but the two guards stopped his advance.

"Get through that doorway!" snapped Pete. "We got work for you to do. March!"

There was nothing for the befuddled Jenkins to do but follow orders. At every turn he was forced to realize he could not escape, so he assisted in straightening up a very dirty, greasy kitchen, hoping by good behavior to gain the guards' confidence.

"My girl friend Cora will miss me if I don't send her a message. I can do that, can't I?" he wheedled with a pleasant smile.

"No!" growled Jack.

Jenkins was visibly shaken. What was back of this terrible scheme of their being held prisoners, he thought nervously. And how long had he been in this place?

"Here's some coffee, Jenkins. Your reward for being the scrubwoman," laughed Pete.

"Thank you," mumbled the chauffeur, gulping down the beverage.

Suddenly he felt very drowsy. He could barely stand. Soon he swayed into the arms of Pete. Unresisting, the man was lugged back to the dark den and bound to the leather sofa.

"Fairweather sure is knocked out," decided Pete after an examination of the older man.

Suddenly a bell sounded and footsteps beat a certain code on the front porch boards.

"Brains is back," announced Jack.

Carefully the den room door was locked as Pete went to let in a tall, slender man. He was laden with bundles.

"Here's your food," said the newcomer softly. "Listen—closely—to—my—orders!"

The two guards huddled closely around the man. As he outlined their job, the man spoke urgently. His scheme meant everything to him; in fact, he seemed to be staking everything on his ability to carry out his strange plan.

"Here is the box," he said finally, pointing to a square wrapped package. "Now I must leave!"

Brains was gone in a flash!

Together the guards shook Thomas Fairweather awake. He argued for his release, even
offering a generous sum for himself and Jenkins' freedom. But Pete and Jack refused to
consider any proposition.

"I have no enemies," cried the wealthy prisoner. "What is this inhuman scheme anyway? Can't you answer a fair question?" he
pleaded.

"No," shouted Pete. "Just take this pen an'
write what we tell you."

"An' no fancy handwritin' either," ordered
Jack, " 'cause we got a sample of your penman-
ship."

"I see," murmured Mr. Fairweather.

The drowsy, stupid feeling was beginning to
leave him; his head was clearing. He took a
fountain pen from his pocket.

A box of fine stationery was opened, a sheet
selected. Firmly the prisoner wrote the words
the two guards dictated. Hastily Pete compared
the script with some on a scrap of paper Brains
had given him.

"Is it okay?" questioned Jack as he prepared
to place an envelope on the table for Mr. Fairweather to address.

"It seems all right," grunted his companion.
"Go ahead."

Clearly, in a bold handwriting, Thomas Fairweather wrote his friend's name.

Captain Ned Krad Dana
Highfort Estate
Ashton.

Tranley and the Dana girls spent the early afternoon of Christmas Eve skiing on a slope not far from the mansion. Louise and Jean thoroughly enjoyed Sonya's brother, who proved to be jolly and gay. He confessed to them that for the past few months he had attended college under the name of Oliver Tranley.

"It was dangerous for me to join Sonya at this time," he revealed. "I came only because we have an important task to accomplish."

Before the young man could say more, the group was startled by the sound of gunfire. The echo came from among the trees only a short distance away.

"What was that?" asked Tranley alertly.

Turning quickly, Jean thought she saw a man dart from some bushes and disappear. Leaving Sonya and her brother behind, the Dana girls hurried through the snow toward the locality from whence the sound had come. Emerging into a small clearing they were greatly relieved at what they saw. Lettie was firing at a target; at least she was trying to do so!

"I guess she'll do no harm this time," Jean chuckled as they watched her. "What do you suppose that man was doing here? He looked as if he were spying," she added soberly.

"We might follow him," suggested Louise. "He may be the jewel thief!"

The Dana girls turned to trail him. The crackle of a stick caused them to pause and glance backward. A huge black bear was lumbering in menacing fashion toward the unsuspecting Lettie!

"Lettie! Lettie!" Jean cried in warning. "Look out!"

The Briggs girl whirled around and saw the approaching animal. Thrown into panic she pulled the trigger of her gun, and the shot went true, wounding the bear but not killing it.

"Now we will have trouble," gasped Louise. "Shoot again, Lettie! Be quick!"

The girl heard the command but was too frightened to obey. Dropping the gun she turned and ran down the trail, the enraged bear in hot pursuit.

"She'll never reach the bungalow in time!" Jean exclaimed fearfully.

Louise recognized that there was only one thing to do. Running forward, she seized the discarded gun. Taking careful aim, she fired a shot.

"Good work, Louise!" praised Jean warmly. "You got him."

The bear had dropped on the snow-covered ground, and was rolling over and over. Louise fired a second shot at close range, putting the animal out of its agony.

Lettie glanced over her shoulder but did not pause. She ran all the way to Tryon's cottage and vanished inside. The sisters returned to the mansion and told their story.

While Captain Dana and Tranley went into the woods to take charge of the dead bear, Louise and Jean had a lengthy chat with Sonya. The girl remarked that she and her brother had expected to arrive at Highfort the previous day but had been delayed.

"We were doing what you call detective work," she said, smiling broadly.

"What sort of detective work?" asked Jean. "You're not looking for Mr. Vitescom?"

"Oh, no, I hope never to see him again. Tranley and I have been trying to trace my lost pin."

"What pin do you mean, Sonya?" inquired Louise. "A valuable one?"

"I hope you will not be distressed that I tell you. It was not your fault."

"What are you trying to say?" Louise asked anxiously.

"It was Tranley who discovered the truth. The star pin which Jean recovered for me—it is not real."

"Not real?" Jean gasped. "It wasn't the one that was stolen?"

Sonya shook her head. "It is what they call a clever imitation. Unless you help me, I fear I never will see our family heirloom again."

CHAPTER XIV

Imitation Jewels

Sonya's words dumbfounded the Danas, for it never had occurred to them that the recovered jewelry was not the original.

"My brother and I talked with the Penfield pawnbroker," the foreign girl resumed her story. "We thought a mistake had been made. He said, 'No,' that this star pin was the same one pawned there days ago by a Maggie Marsh."

Sonya drew the brooch from her pocket. Jean took one glance at the cheap glass stones and protested:

"But is this the pin I recovered? It doesn't look like it."

"The pawnbroker insists it is the same. He said the one brought to him had no great value," the girl replied.

"You questioned him about Maggie Marsh?" Louise asked curiously.

"My brother did. The girl was young, about our own age. He said she talked in a very boastful way."

Louise and Jean were convinced that Lettie Briggs was the one person who might explain the pawnshop mystery. Now the affair had reached really serious proportions. No longer was it a schoolgirl prank which they had overlooked and almost forgotten in the excitement at Highfort.

Without revealing their purpose to Sonya, they went presently to Tryon's cabin, intending to question the suspected girl and find out if she were guilty. Lettie met them at the door.

"Did you bring my cousin's gun?" she asked before they could speak. "I left it in the woods and I don't want to go after it alone. I might meet another bear."

"I took the gun to the house," said Louise.

"We'll walk back with you to get it, Lettie," Jean suggested quickly. "Get into some warm clothes because it's snowing."

The excursion offered the Dana girls an opportunity to talk privately with Lettie. Going straight to the point they told her of the substitution which had been made in the valuable jeweled pin.

"We know that you were the one who pawned it," Jean said bluntly. "You took the name of your mother's maid, Maggie Marsh. Since the real pin is still missing you must realize that you're liable to arrest."

"I don't know anything about Sonya's silly old pin," Lettie retorted, but it was plain to see she was frightened.

"Perhaps you'll talk if the sheriff questions you," Louise warned her.

"Don't call him," said the girl in sudden panic. "I'll tell you all about it."

"Then you did pawn the pin?" Louise questioned her intently.

"I got our maid to do it when she came to school. She didn't know it wasn't mine. I was afraid to leave it at school for fear it would be found. I saw it lying on your desk at Starhurst. I only meant it in fun. I thought it would embarrass you."

"Maggie didn't substitute another pin when she took it to Penfield?"

"Oh no, she came right back. She couldn't have found one just like it so quickly. I didn't know it was valuable, and I didn't mean to steal it. It was only a joke."

"An expensive joke for Sonya. The star jewel cannot be replaced," Louise impressed upon Lettie.

"You won't let her send me to jail, will you? I'll do anything I can to help get it back again," the Briggs girl wailed.

So sincere did the girl seem, the Danas felt that she was telling the truth. She should be made to realize, however, she was involved in a very serious affair.

"Will you tell your father the entire story?" Jean interposed sternly.

"Yes, I'll explain to him," Lettie promised. "I'll ask him to pay Sonya for the pin if she doesn't find it."

Since the girl seemed so contrite, Louise and Jean took pity upon her. A few minutes later they left her at the log bungalow, reminding her not to forget the agreement.

"Father is inside," Lettie responded. "I'll tell him right away."

Louise and Jean had no reason to doubt that Lettie would keep her promise. They were amazed, therefore, at the words which reached their ears. The walls of the cabin were not soundproof, and as they walked slowly away they heard Lettie's shrill, penetrating voice.

"Oh, Father," she was saying, "I can't endure another day at Highfort. There's nothing to do here, and I'm lonesome for my mother. Can't we start home tonight?"

Jean and Louise gazed at each other in disgust. It was perfectly evident that Lettie had no intention of telling her father the truth. Well, maybe he would find it out from the police.

The sisters found their Uncle Ned in the living room of the mansion feeling very depressed. Before they could speak to him, Tryon came in from the hall.

"Here is a letter I brought from the post-office, Captain Dana," he said.

Taking it eagerly, the older man looked at the envelope. A puzzled expression came into the skipper's eyes. "This looks like Tom Fair-weather's writing, but I don't understand...."

"Open it up, Uncle, please," begged Jean impetuously. "We're breathless to know what it says."

Ripping the envelope, the old sea captain read aloud.

"Dear Ned: Since important business detains me elsewhere, I'm forced to ask you and your family to vacate the mansion. I will see you in Oak Falls before long and explain everything.

Very sincerely,
Tom Fairweather."

Aunt Harriet had entered the room and at the conclusion of the reading she said forcefully, "That answers the big question. Now we will start for home."

"But there's a mistake here," replied her brother slowly. "Look at the middle name on this envelope—Krad—I haven't any such name." The sea captain gazed fixedly at the mysterious insertion.

"It is strange," murmured Louise, voicing the sentiments of all in the group.

Suddenly Jean gave an excited whoop. "I have an idea. I just figured out that 'Krad' spells 'dark' backwards." Three pair of eyes focused on the younger Dana girl as she continued, " 'Ned' could be 'den'. . . ."

"Dark den!" cried Louise. "You're a whiz, Jean!" exulted her sister.

The captain stared in silence. Could it be true? What had befallen his friend, and was Jenkins involved?

"It's someone trying to get us out of this place. He has forced Fairweather to write this," thundered the old sailor. "We'll stay right here and bend every effort to trace down the scoundrel who is holding my friend."

"I'm so glad," seconded Jean. "We won't give up the ship, Uncle Ned!"

"We'll show the villain he can't frighten the Danas so easily. Henceforth we'll redouble our efforts to aid Tom. 'Dark den.' It sounds worse than the brig," concluded the captain as he paced the floor with a heavy scowl on his fine features.

"I'll report this at once to the police," he announced and went off in the car.

Soon after he had gone the sisters heard the tinkle of bells at a distance and hurried to a window to look out. Two sprightly black horses, pulling a sleigh, trotted down the road. The Danas were astonished to see that Tranley held the reins. At that moment Sonya came down the stairs, muffled in furs.

"Will you ride with us?" their schoolmate invited the girls cordially.

With their minds still on the mysterious message, it was hard for them to put their thoughts on anything else. They did not reply at once.

"In our country it is an old custom to distribute food and gifts to deserving folks," explained Sonya. "Tranley has a list of worthy persons living near Indian Mountain. We go now to take them presents."

"How very thoughtful of you!" Louise exclaimed, deeply impressed.

"I think I should like to go," said Jean. "Come on, Louise."

The next hour was spent in calling at the homes of poor families living close by. The Olavus distributed toys to children, and in not one case did anyone take offense, for the aristocratic couple were so gracious their charity was gratefully accepted.

Long shadows fell across the road as the gay party started back toward Highfort. As the sleigh wound through a dense woods, there suddenly was a terrific crash not far away. Immediately the high-spirited horses bolted, starting down the twisting road at breakneck speed.

"Whoa!" shouted Tranley, pulling hard on the reins. "Whoa!"

Little by little he began to regain control of them, but it was almost impossible to guide the frightened team. He could only keep the horses as nearly as possible to the center of the road. Sonya clung in terror to his arm, making his work more difficult.

Suddenly the vehicle was carried over a large rock which lay half hidden beneath the snow.

The Dana girls in the back seat felt themselves tilted sideways.

"Hold on!" shouted Tranley, bracing his feet. "Hold on!"

Louise and Jean clutched frantically for support but could find none. Another sideways swerve and out they pitched into a deep snowbank. Swinging onto its runner again, the sleigh went crazily down the road.

Recovering from the shock a few moments later, Jean looked around but could not see her sister anywhere.

"Louise!" she called. "Louise!"

There was no response, but presently Jean saw a huddled, motionless body lying a few feet away. Staggering through the deep snow, she reached her sister's side.

"Louise, are you hurt?" she asked frantically. "Answer me—speak!"

Louise stirred slightly and opened her eyes. "I'm all r-right. How about you?"

Neither of the girls had been hurt much. One of Jean's elbows, which had struck a buried rock, was slightly skinned, and Louise had been momentarily stunned, but upon the whole they felt that their fall had been an easy one, thanks to the deep snow.

After resting several minutes, the girls trudged along the road side by side in the gathering dusk. They hoped that Tranley and his sister soon would return for them, but minutes passed without a glimpse of the sleigh, so they took a short cut through the woods.

"What an odd shape the fort has when seen from this direction," Louise remarked, pausing to catch her breath as they neared the mansion.

"I guess we never really took a good look at it except from the inside," added Jean. "I know I never noticed that long wing before."

"It must contain the service unit—laundry and storerooms."

Knowing that within a few minutes it would be quite dark, the girls hastened their steps. They had not gone far when Jean suddenly paused and grabbed her sister's arm.

"Look, Louise!" she cried in astonishment.

"Where?"

"The roof of the service wing!"

"I don't see anything."

"Neither do I now, Louise. But it was there when I spoke. Something was moving on the roof. I'm sure it was a man."

Louise regarded her sister with interest. "Perhaps the jewel thief!"

CHAPTER XV

A Call for Help

The two girls hastened their steps. Reaching the building, they raced around it but could see no evidence of any way in which a person could have climbed up or down from the roof. There was no ladder, no steps, no vines.

"We know he couldn't come down the chimney," said Louise, "so how did he get away? Oh dear, he has slipped through our fingers again," she sighed.

At this moment Sonya and her brother arrived, glad to find the girls unhurt. After apologizing for the mishap, their classmate said she would like to fix one more thing for Christmas. Mysteriously she led them all to the kitchen.

"I will make an animated gingerbread man," she announced. "I learned the secret in my own country from a recipe contained in an old fairy tale."

At this remark Applecore looked darkly at the speaker. She did not like the presence of the Olavus and now she was frightened with this idea. Grudgingly she brought the ingredients while Tranley hunted for some thin wire.

"I don't believe Cora ever baked a gingerbread man such as mine," said Sonya pleasantly. "He will walk—right out of the oven!" she added, as she put the pan into the stove about ten minutes later.

She closely watched the hands of the clock, refusing to peep inside the oven until the proper moment had arrived to remove the goody. Then throwing open the door, she seized a strand of wire which had been cleverly inserted in the dough and which Cora had failed to observe. The maid's eyes widened as the little gingerbread man hopped from the baking pan to the stove door.

"It's hot in here," he squeaked in a high-pitched voice. "I want to get out!"

Punctuating his words, the little fellow leaped down from his perch, hopping toward Cora Appel.

"Help! Lemme out o' here!" the maid shrieked, backing away. "Witches has been at work!"

In the meantime Marybelle had come in and she too was alarmed by the antics of the gingerbread man. Both she and Cora were convinced that Sonya had supernatural powers, although the Dana girls attempted to explain there was nothing to fear.

"Don't be frightened," soothed Sonya, laying down the toy. "You see, it's all what you call a joke. Unless I pull the wire, Mr. Gingerbread cannot walk."

"But he talked! He said it was hot in the oven!" exclaimed Cora. "Oh, the woman is a witch!" she cried, and the two maids fled from the room.

"That was a clever trick of ventriloquism on your part," Louise told Sonya.

"Yes, I threw my voice to make it seem that the gingerbread man said the words, but I'm afraid I overplayed the joke."

Despite explanations, Cora was not satisfied and distrusted Sonya. Thus the difficult situation in the house was made even more tense. Suspicion was growing on all sides.

Soon after dinner Louise and Jean began to look for Lettie, although in truth they were sorry they had invited her to the mansion for Christmas Eve. After an hour elapsed and still she did not come, they decided perhaps she had gone home, or else was too frightened of what the Dana girls might tell the police to show up. So they started the festivities without her.

Fresh logs were piled high on the hearth and the entire household gathered about the living room fireplace. Even Mrs. Plimpton forgot her grievances and joined in the singing of old songs. Fruit cake was served, and Captain Dana's toast to Saint Nicholas was drunk in hot chocolate.

As the final event, empty stockings were hung by the fireplace and Louise told the story of the origin of the custom. It was with difficulty that

Sonya, Tranley and Marybelle were induced to join in the ceremony. Their reluctance added to the enjoyment of Uncle Ned and Aunt Harriet, who would stay up a little longer than the others for their part in the activities.

"This is going to be a nice Christmas despite everything," Louise remarked as she and Jean got ready for bed just after midnight.

"But a strange one," added her sister. "Here we are in a house claimed by three different parties. Mr. Fairweather is missing; Sonya lost a valuable pin and got an imitation one in its place; Mrs. Plimpton's jewels have been stolen; and the Olavus's enemy Vitescom has been seen near here."

"Everything to worry us," agreed Louise.

Hardly were the words out of her mouth when steps sounded outside and there was a loud knock on the front door. Job Tryon tramped into the hall, carefully brushing snow from his overshoes.

"I've just had a strange telephone message," he announced. "It worries me."

At the sound of the disturbance downstairs Jean and Louise donned robes and slippers and came to the top of the steps. Both shared the thought that perhaps at last Mr. Fairweather had come. They were startled to see the caretaker at this hour of the night and more surprised at his words.

"I'm very worried," he explained in a

strained voice. "About ten minutes ago I was roused out of bed to answer the phone. A weak voice from far away said, 'Tryon, come help me!'"

"Was there anything else?" asked Captain Dana.

"Yes, but it didn't make sense. This was what I heard, though. 'Fairweather—prisoner—Hunter's Island—tell Danas mysterious fireplace——'"

"Our name was mentioned and Fairweather's?" Uncle Ned asked excitedly. "You're sure?"

"Oh, yes, sir. Then the connection was broken. I don't think there's much sense to it, but I thought I'd better tell you."

"You did right to come straight to us. But the question is, what can we do?" mused the captain.

By this time the girls had reached the first floor and were listening intently.

"Perhaps Mr. Fairweather is being held a prisoner near here in a dark den," suggested Jean, eagerly. "At a place called Hunter's Island!"

"There's no spot by that name around these parts," said the caretaker. "To make sure I called State Trooper Fuller and asked him."

"I've heard of various islands in that big lake near here," mentioned Captain Dana.

"Oh yes, sir, there are plenty of them. Dozens of 'em. But none called that."

"Do you know of one where a hunter would be likely to go for some special kind of shooting?" asked Jean.

"One place would be about as good as another for shootin'," Job Tryon replied.

"Uncle Ned, I know how the search for Mr. Fairweather might be narrowed!" exclaimed Louise suddenly.

"How?" inquired the captain.

"Couldn't we limit it to islands having telephone facilities?"

"Yes, that's a good suggestion, Louise. I'll get ready at once and go with Tryon. From his cabin we'll call up the troopers and have a searching party organized."

Jean and Louise were eager to accompany the men, but Miss Dana pointed out there was nothing they could do. While awaiting their uncle's return, the girls discussed the strange telephone message.

"What could have been meant by 'Tell Danas mysterious fireplace,'" Louise mused, chin cushioned on her drawn-up knees.

"Maybe Fairweather and Jenkins actually are imprisoned inside a fireplace, not a dark den!" said Jean, who could figure out nothing else from the strange message Tryon had received.

"In the chimney, you mean?" Miss Dana gasped.

"Couldn't it be possible?" asked Jean, addressing Louise.

"According to the book I read, some of the ancient fireplaces had hiding places in them," Louise admitted thoughtfully.

Uncle Ned returned in a short time, saying the troopers were at work on the case. Throughout the rest of the night there were no disturbances at Highfort and the household slept, if not peacefully, at least exhausted. Christmas Day dawned gray and cheerless.

"What's the use of trying to celebrate?" Jean said drearily. "If only we had good news of Mr. Fairweather everything would seem better."

"The police are doing everything possible," said Miss Dana. "I think we should go through with our little program exactly as we planned it. First, let's see what old Saint Nicholas left in the stockings."

Spurred on by their aunt, Louise and Jean made a pretense of being lighthearted. With Sonya, Tranley, Marybelle and Cora they went to the fireplace where the empty stockings had been hung.

"Santa has been here!" laughed Jean. "Every stocking bulges! Unpack yours first, Applecore. Please hurry."

Obediently the maid removed the uppermost

tissue-wrapped package. The package fell away to reveal a collection of dime store china.

"Dishes," she wailed. "There ain't nothin' in the world I hate worse'n dishes! You always have to wash 'em, and unless you're real careful they're always flyin' out o' your hand and goin' crash!"

There were other packages in her stocking, including a silver pin and material for a silk dress. Cora's pleasure was so great upon seeing the additional gifts that she was able to laugh and forget about the joke which had hinted of her dish-breaking habit.

Tranley and Sonya enjoyed the fun-making presents they found and were very grateful for books and candy. They thanked "Santa" over and over.

Jean's turn came next. She found her stocking filled with a number of knick-knacks while Aunt Harriet had included an envelope of money. This was indeed a very welcome gift.

"I'm sorry I couldn't buy anything," she apologized. "I thought you might get what you want most, Jean."

The only remaining stocking belonged to Louise. A dime store fingerprint set caused considerable laughter and from Uncle Ned she received an autographed volume of her favorite author's writings. In the toe of the stocking was an envelope similar to the one Jean had received.

"I know what I'll do with my money," Louise said, smiling at Aunt Harriet. "I shall buy a new pair of ice skates."

As she spoke, she tore open the envelope. It contained not money, but a folded sheet of brown wrapping paper.

"How queer!" exclaimed Miss Dana, a mystified look on her face. "Why, someone must have taken the bills I put in that envelope!" She was so puzzled she could say nothing further at the moment.

Louise Dana unfolded the piece of paper gingerly. There, across its surface in uneven lines, had been pasted several letters cut from newspaper headlines. The following message was spelled out:

"YOU AND FAMILY LEAVE THIS HOUSE AT ONCE OR SUFFER PEN-ALTY. THIS IS YOUR ONLY WARN-ING."

CHAPTER XVI

A Hoax

At a glance Jean too read the strange message and offered it to Miss Dana.

"This must be your little joke, Aunt Harriet," she said, her eyes questioning.

"I played no joke," replied her aunt. "I tucked an envelope of money the same as yours into Louise's stocking."

"Then someone must have removed it and substituted this paper!"

As she spoke, Louise gazed from one face to another, trying to discern the guilty person. Everyone seemed as astonished by the mysterious note as she herself.

"The threat is intended seriously, I believe," declared Miss Dana. "Who could have sent it, and why?"

Louise and Jean had very little to say in the presence of the others. Privately they discussed whether or not Mrs. Plimpton or Mary-belle might have been responsible.

"Neither of them acts guilty," declared Jean. "Anyway, I can't think of any reason why they would resort to such a trick."

"Mrs. Plimpton is eager to get rid of us,"

argued her sister. "She might have hoped to frighten us."

"True, Jean, but I have a feeling the message is more serious than that."

Later in the morning the girls tramped to Tryon's bungalow and found Lettie Briggs still there. In the course of the conversation they mentioned the threatening message found in Louise's stocking. A faint smile, instantly noted by the Dana sisters, played over the girl's face.

"I don't suppose you know anything about the matter?" Jean asked her suspiciously.

"How should I?"

"You look as if you did."

"Do I?" Lettie grinned in a provoking way. "Maybe I have learned something you'd like to hear. What will you give me if I solve the mystery of Highfort for you?"

"Our highest praise," replied Louise.

"Will you forget about Sonya's pin?"

"We'll make things as easy for you as we can," Jean promised reluctantly. "Please tell us what you know about the strange note."

"Oh, I don't know anything yet. But I should have information for you soon."

Refusing to tell more, Lettie airily said good-bye to the Dana girls. Motoring into the village, she sent a telegram to her friend, Holweg Trout, requesting him to come without delay to Highfort.

Unaware of the action of the Briggs girl, Louise and Jean anxiously awaited news from their uncle and Job Tryon, who had gone to help in the search for Mr. Fairweather. Shortly before noon the two men drove into the grounds. Weary and discouraged, they reported that the troopers had found no trace of the missing man.

"Men still are combing the islands," Captain Dana told the girls. "However, the task looks rather hopeless. I am convinced that Fairweather has met serious trouble," continued Uncle Ned. "I wish I could think of some way to trace him."

Although a deep shadow hovered over Highfort, Christmas Day was not lacking in gaiety. Wisely the Danas had not told Cora about the alarming message delivered by the caretaker. Instead they led her to believe that Jenkins soon would be found.

Happy in the thought, the girl sang at her work. She cooked an excellent holiday meal and served it well. Even Mrs. Plimpton declared that a better turkey had never been tasted.

"Miss Daisy seems to have experienced a change of heart," Louise remarked to her sister later. "Actually she's tried to be friendly today."

"Almost too friendly," said Jean with a sniff. "You know, somehow I don't trust her actions," she added.

Could the Dana girls have penetrated her bedroom wall they might have been truly alarmed, for at that particular moment Mrs. Plimpton was packing jewelry into a mailing carton.

"I wish you to take this box to the post office at once, Marybelle," she ordered her maid. "There are plenty of stamps on it. If my plan works, I'll be rid of the Olavus and possibly the Danas as well!"

"You're sending all the rest of your jewelry home, Miss Daisy!" the maid exclaimed in faint protest.

"Certainly. Mind you don't breathe a word about it to anyone. If I accuse the Olavus of stealing it, they'll become frightened and leave," she said in triumph.

"But that's dishonest, Miss Daisy!"

"It's not dishonest to get rid of folks who are trying to steal my home, is it?"

"They have a claim too——"

"Are you working for them or for me?" Mrs. Plimpton spoke tartly and thrust several letters into the maid's hand. "Mail these while you're in town," she commanded arrogantly.

Marybelle glanced at the writing in surprise.

"Why, Miss Daisy, you've disguised your hand!" she exclaimed.

"Never mind," the widow declared impatiently. "Do as you're told and don't ask questions. I'll handle this matter in my own way."

Marybelle lapsed into silence but Mrs. Plimpton could not still the maid's thoughts so easily.

"It was Miss Daisy who put the warning note in Louise's Christmas stocking!" the girl told herself. "If she gets too high and mighty with me maybe I'll tell what I know!"

In another part of the mansion a second conversation which concerned the Dana girls was under way. Earnestly Tranley Olavu was arguing with his sister.

"I like Louise and Jean as well as you do, Sonya. But you must realize we can't carry out our plan while they are here."

"I cannot ask them to leave, Tranley. It would be rude. They would not understand."

"You must use diplomacy, Sonya. You will do as I ask?"

"If I must," sighed his sister, "but it does grieve me to hurt kind friends."

Unaware that they had become a target of intrigue, Louise and Jean spent the late afternoon on the ski slopes. By the time they returned to the house, the evening meal was over so they saw neither the Olavus nor Mrs. Plimpton. Lunching alone in the kitchen they talked in low tones.

"Christmas is past now," said Louise. "Or will be at midnight. I think we should buckle down and solve the mysteries connected with this place."

Jean reached for her third turkey sandwich and a second glass of milk. "First thing in the morning," she agreed.

The girls went to their room. For half an hour they could hear people stirring about, then the household settled for the night. There was complete silence indoors and out.

To Jean's annoyance Louise could not sleep. She kept rolling over, first one direction, then another.

"Say, what's the matter with you?"

"Nothing. I'm just too tense to sleep. This awful quiet almost seems like a stage setting for some strange happening."

For some time Louise remained motionless and Jean dropped off to sleep. Then suddenly the older girl swung her feet out of bed and reached for her slippers. Her sister awoke at once.

"I can't lie here another instant," Louise said in a whisper. "Maybe it's imagination but I keep thinking I hear the floor downstairs squeaking."

"Oh, you're silly—" Jean began, only to break off. "—Why, I hear someone moving about in the living room! I really do!"

She too got out of bed and slipped a flashlight into her bathrobe pocket. Side by side the girls tiptoed along the dark hall and descended the stairs. They heard no alarming sound, but unexpectedly a beam of bright light moved across the ceiling in the living room.

"It's someone with a flashlight!" Jean whispered, gripping Louise's hand.

CHAPTER XVII

Warning Notes

As the girls remained motionless, they could hear the intruder moving stealthily about in the living room of the mansion.

"Let's see who it is," whispered Louise, stealing forward. "Careful! It won't do for us to be caught."

Taking care to avoid stepping on loose boards, the girls tiptoed to the doorway. A tall, slender man stood with his back toward them. As they watched him, he knelt before the fireplace and apparently examined the flue.

"Who is he?" Jean whispered tensely.

The question was answered for her as the man straightened up and turned slightly. He was Tranley Olavu!

"Maybe he's looking for a burglar too," Jean suggested in her sister's ear. "Ought we to speak to him?"

Louise shook her head. There seemed to be several reasons for keeping the matter a secret.

"One doesn't search for a burglar up a chimney," she whispered back.

"Then what is he doing?"

"I wish I knew, Jean. Perhaps he is looking for something hidden——"

Tranley put an abrupt end to the whispered conversation by walking directly toward the girls. They barely had time to take refuge before he passed through the hall and tiptoed up the stairway.

"Let's look at that fireplace ourselves," Louise proposed eagerly.

Crossing the room, she stooped to throw the flashlight beam far up the flue. Neither of the girls could discover anything unusual about its construction.

The fireplace itself was modern, the flue small, with walls of common firebrick. Although the girls groped about, they could find no loose bricks, ash pits, secret niches, or for that matter, anything to make it of particular interest.

"I can't understand what Tranley was doing here," Louise said, puzzled, settling back on her heels. "All this old fireplace has in it is soot!"

"Plenty of that," laughed Jean softly. "You're as black as if you were corked up for a minstrel show! You ought to see your face!"

"Take a glance at yourself," Louise countered. "You look like a black ghost flitting in the moonlight."

Satisfied that they could learn nothing more at this time and still mystified about the actions of young Olavu, the girls tiptoed toward their room. They were not as quiet as they believed, for the door of Mrs. Plimpton's quarters suddenly swung open.

"Who is there?" she called in a quavering voice. "Who is making a disturbance?"

Jean and Louise remained motionless. They might have avoided detection had not the widow directed the beam of a flashlight full upon them. To her horrified gaze they were revealed as black spooks.

"Help! Help!" she shrieked, dropping the flashlight and slamming and locking her door.

During the moment of darkness, Jean and Louise darted into their own room. In a twinkling they had changed their blackened pajamas for nightgowns and had washed their hands and faces.

Fifteen minutes later Miss Dana, who had been excitedly summoned by the widow, found her nieces to all purposes sleeping peacefully in their bed.

"Get up, girls," she urged, pulling back the covers. "Mrs. Plimpton says strange black figures tried to break into the house. I don't want to awaken your Uncle Ned—he needs his rest so badly."

"Don't you believe what she said, Aunt Harriet," chuckled Jean with a wink.

Miss Dana gazed suspiciously at her nieces. They had not been sleeping at all, she was quite certain. What was the reason?

"Ask us no questions, we'll tell you no lies,"

Louise warbled, trying to forestall her aunt.

"I rather thought you girls might know something about the matter," their relative laughed. "But I'll wait for you to explain in your own good time."

At breakfast Mrs. Plimpton assumed the limelight with a graphic account of her midnight encounter with the two ebony spooks. Jean and Louise listened soberly, keeping their faces composed even though they knew Miss Dana was watching them closely.

"No one pays any attention to me in this house—my own home too!" the widow complained. "You needn't believe it, but I tell you I know someone was prowling about here last night! This place gives me the creeps."

The Dana girls stole a quick glance at Tranley. His eyes were upon his plate, but it was evident that he was ill at ease.

Breakfast over, the young man drew his sister aside for a quiet talk. Immediately thereafter he sought out Mrs. Plimpton, telling her firmly that he thought she should leave Highfort now that Christmas was past.

"Who are you to order me about?" the widow demanded in a voice so loud it could be heard in every room. "Young man, I'll have you know that Highfort belongs to me——"

"Our claim is just and can be proved in court," Tranley interrupted. "Sonya and I did

not wish to ask you to leave until after the holiday, but now we must.''

"I won't go!" Mrs. Plimpton fairly screamed.
"Wild horses can't drive me from here. Oh!
Oh! You dreadful, cruel man! You've brought
on another one of my heart attacks.''

Leaning heavily on the arm of Marybelle, she
staggered to her room and to bed. A whiff of
smelling salts and recollection of her plan for
staying soon revived the woman.

Louise, Jean and Sonya were not witnesses to
the scene, for immediately after breakfast they
had motored to town in the Dana car. Supplies
were purchased, then a stop was made at the
post office for mail.

To the surprise of the Dana girls they received identical appearing letters, each post-
marked at the local station. Jean hastily tore
hers open and exclaimed:

"It's another threatening message! I am
warned to leave Highfort at once!''

"Mine says the same thing!" cried Louise as
she read her own letter. "Well, of all things!
Who sent them?''

"It looks like a woman's handwriting. She
signs herself 'A Friend.' ''

For a moment Sonya said nothing as the girls
showed her the two letters. Then to the amazement of Louise and Jean she declared soberly:

"Perhaps the writer does mean to be friendly.

Maybe it is best that you leave Highfort.''

The Dana girls regarded their schoolmate in blank astonishment. They could not believe that she actually wished them to go away.

"Oh, we're not afraid," said Louise. "It would take more than a threatening letter to frighten us."

"I think you should leave," Sonya repeated, looking at the ground. "Not only are you in danger, but you gain nothing by remaining. Perhaps you do harm."

"Do you and your brother plan to leave this place soon?" asked Jean.

"No, Highfort is our home. We must stay here—at least until our schools open."

The subject was allowed to drop, but Louise and Jean were puzzled by Sonya's attitude. She seemed to have changed completely in her manner. On their way to the troopers' headquarters, after leaving her at a small department store, the Danas discussed the situation.

"She does not seem to be as friendly in her feeling toward us, Jean."

"Yes," agreed Jean, absently plucking an icicle from a tree branch overhead, "it's obvious she wants us to leave Highfort. But why? I can't understand it."

"I'll venture to bet that Tranley is behind the whole thing."

"He seemed to like us at first."

"I think that he still does, Louise, but for

some reason we're in the way. He may be after something which is hidden at Highfort!''

"I have another idea!" exclaimed Louise. "You recall that just as Sonya was leaving Starhurst she hinted she might hide the Olavu jewels in a mysterious fireplace?"

"Yes, I do. Surely you don't think——"

"That she and her brother have selected the living room fireplace at the mansion," Louise completed her theory quickly. "Yes, Jean, I was thinking exactly that."

"But it would be such a stupid place! The jewels easily could be stolen."

"It would be a very unsafe place in my opinion. Let's ask her about it, Jean, and in a tactful way advise against such a move. If my guess is right, we may be real friends to her and her brother."

The girls had arrived at the office of the state troopers. Disappointing news awaited them there, for they learned that searching parties of police had found no trace of the missing Fairweather car or its occupants. Every island in the vicinity, with and without a telephone, had been visited. There was no clue to the two missing men.

"I'm beginning to believe that Job Tryon did not get the message straight," Jean declared as the girls returned to their car. "If the telephone connection was poor, he may not have heard the words exactly as they were spoken."

"The fact remains that Fairweather and Jenkins are missing," Louise replied. "Until they are found, we must work further on what information we have."

Sonya awaited the girls in the parked automobile. As they drove slowly out of town, she had little to say. Louise and Jean, hurt by their friend's attitude, likewise remained silent.

At the edge of town a group of children were coasting on a near-by hill. Unexpectedly one of the sleds, breaking a new track, glided through a hole in the barrier fence and swerved straight into the path of the oncoming sedan.

"That child!" screamed Sonya, every muscle tensing. "He'll be killed!"

Jean, who was at the wheel, dared not apply brakes on the icy road. To do so would throw the car into a disastrous skid. Instead, she steered as close as she could to the ditch, missing the child by inches.

"That was marvelous driving, Jean!" Louise praised her sister warmly.

The girls stopped by the roadside to glance back. Unharmed, the lad on the sled could be seen coasting through a field on the opposite side of the road.

"My life was saved in a similar way when I was a child," Sonya said shakily. "Never will I forget it."

As the journey was resumed, Louise and Jean promptly forgot the incident, but their friend

could not. She seemed unusually nervous and
upset. They assumed that her strange attitude
was the result of the near accident. Therefore, it came as a distinct surprise when the girl
said abruptly:

"I am so ashamed of myself. So very
ashamed."

"Why should you be?" inquired Louise in
astonishment.

"You do not understand. My brother and I
have kept a secret from you."

"A secret?" Louise's pulse quickened, for
she felt that the girl was on the verge of revealing some important information.

"Yes," Sonya responded soberly. "As soon
as we reach Highfort I'll talk with Tranley. If
he grants permission, then I shall tell you."

CHAPTER XVIII

The Olavu Secret

ALTHOUGH the Dana girls waited hopefully, Sonya had nothing more to say. She lapsed into a moody silence, which finally became embarrassing. At length, in an effort to stimulate conversation, Louise remarked:

"I suppose it seems strange to you, Sonya, that our family remains at Highfort. But we were here first at the invitation of a man who bought the place in good faith. Naturally we're worried about Mr. Fairweather, and Uncle Ned feels we should stay to protect his interests."

"I understand," nodded their classmate, her eyes on the ribbon of road. "If I were in your place, I would do the same."

This response, which seemed to contradict the girl's previous words, left Louise and Jean more bewildered than before. They could not fathom Sonya's motives. Did she really wish them to leave Highfort?

"Oh, by the way," Louise said carelessly, "whatever became of those family jewels you took from Starhurst? Have you found a safe hiding place for them yet?"

Sonya shook her head. "Tranley will hide

154

the jewels as soon as the star pin has been recovered," she replied quietly.

"Isn't it dangerous to wait?"

"Tranley does not think so," Sonya spoke
briefly, making it plain that she preferred not
to discuss the matter any further.

When they arrived at Highfort the girls
found that an unpleasant situation had developed. No sooner had the three friends entered
the mansion than they heard Mrs. Plimpton's
shrill voice in the living room proclaiming that
she had again been robbed.

"All my jewels are gone!" she wailed. "Who
took them? It was that Olavu girl and her
brother! The other night I heard him sneak-
ing around the house when he thought I was
asleep! Unless they leave here at once I'll call
the sheriff! This time I'll really do it!"

The Danas were astounded. Sonya became
deathly pale. As the girls walked into the room
they found Captain Dana, Aunt Harriet and
young Olavu present.

"If you have finished, Mrs. Plimpton, I'd like
to say something," interposed Tranley in a
quiet voice. "My sister and I know nothing
about your lost jewelry. But I feel that it
would be best if I call a lawyer and have him
talk with you."

"A lawyer?" the widow quavered. "No,
don't do that. We can settle this ourselves."

"As far as I am concerned it is settled now.

Sonya and I did *not* steal your jewels! We'll talk no more about it.''

Despite the seriousness of the charge, it was almost amusing to see Mrs. Plimpton scurry to her room. Nevertheless, not only was her accusation serious but the whole matter of missing jewels took on fresh significance. In a very unexpected manner the Dana girls came upon a clue to this latest angle of the mystery.

While looking outdoors for any evidence which might have been left by a thief, they noticed Lettie Briggs looking into one of the windows. Glancing around, she saw the sisters staring at her and became very flustered.

"Anything you'd like to know?" asked Jean.

"Why—uh—no, no thanks," replied the peeper. Recovering herself she added, "This is a very interesting building, isn't it?"

"Yes, it is," agreed Louise. "Would you like to come in?"

"I guess I better not," said Lettie. "That girl Marybelle doesn't like me."

"I didn't know you'd met her," Jean spoke up, surprised.

Lettie went on to explain that she had asked the maid some questions about herself and Mrs. Plimpton when she had seen her at the post office Christmas afternoon. She said that the maid was putting a small package and two letters into the box at the time and seemed to be afraid Lettie would see the addresses on them.

"Marybelle is a very impudent person," concluded the Briggs girl, stalking away.

The Danas had their own ideas on this score, yet they could imagine the maid's annoyance at being questioned by a stranger. In the conversation between the sisters which followed the theory was evolved that there might be some connection with Marybelle's presence at the postbox and the story of the missing jewels. Could the girl have stolen them and sent them away?

"Let's question her," suggested Jean.

When sought out and taken alone into a small library of the mansion, Marybelle would reveal nothing about the name and address on the package. Finally Louise told her quietly that should the police come they would suspect her at once. Suddenly the girl began to cry and between sobs said:

"I'll tell you everything—everything. I hate this place and—and I h-hate Mrs. Plimpton. The only reason I stay with her is because she pays me well."

Marybelle fumbled for a handkerchief and blew her nose. Then she continued her story of unhappy days with the widow and ended with a startling confession about the jewels having been mailed.

"She wanted to make Mr. Tranley and his

sister leave, and she's going to make you go, too. That's why she sent you the threatening letters."

Here was news!

"Marybelle, we are very glad you told us and we shall not give you away to your mistress," said Louise kindly. "We are sorry we suspected you. Now please answer one more question. It may explain some of the strange happenings around this mansion."

"I'll tell you anything," offered the maid. "I don't care what happens here, 'cause I'm not going to stay any longer! I hate it!"

"Was the story of your other jewel robbery a hoax?" asked Louise. "When the diamond ring was taken."

"Oh, no, those things really were stolen. And I think somebody entered Mrs. Plimpton's room again later trying to take more jewelry. I found her bags open and things strewn around one afternoon. I didn't tell her 'cause she gets mad so easy. Maybe you think she put that warning note in the stocking, but she didn't. But I guess it gave her the idea about threatening letters."

The Danas felt the girl was telling the truth and now steered the conversation in to another channel. After impressing Marybelle with the seriousness of her mistress's deception and accusation of the Olavus, they suggested it would be far better for the widow to leave Highfort.

"It is very doubtful if she has any claim on the place," said Louise. "Furthermore, matters here are getting worse. Will you please talk to Mrs. Plimpton and urge her to go away?"

"I certainly will," agreed Marybelle. "If I tell her *I'm* going, I bet she won't stay without me."

As she left to seek out the widow, Jean and Louise went to their aunt and whispered their latest findings. Their relative was glad one mystery was solved, but none the less worried about the still unexplained happenings.

"In the meantime life goes on the same," she sighed. "This is a strange world. Well, girls, I've just baked two pies and I think one of them might be appreciated at the Tryon bungalow. Will you take it over?"

The sisters presented themselves at the door of the cabin. Before they could knock, they heard loud voices from inside. Lettie was talking to Mr. Briggs, protesting that she did not wish to return home.

"But, Father," they heard her say, "my biggest mystery case is about to break! I can't leave Highfort now."

"Mystery case! Tommyrot!" Mr. Briggs exclaimed impatiently. "All week you've been begging to go home. And now when I'm ready you want to stay."

"I've changed my mind. I am expecting **De**tective Trout at any time, Father. You won't ask me to go without seeing him?"

"I've had about enough of your detective escapades, Lettie. They all end the same way."

"You're being unfair," his daughter accused him, breaking into tears. "This is the biggest chance I ever had in my life."

"Just to humor you I'll give you one more day here," Mr. Briggs said wearily. "But only one, remember that."

The Dana girls were embarrassed to enter just now, so they retreated a hundred yards from the cabin, then again approached. This time they warbled a Starhurst song which would serve to warn Lettie. They were quite right in their guess, for all was serene when they knocked on the front door. The girl opened it herself to admit them.

"Hello," she said in surprise. "I didn't expect to see you so soon again."

"We brought a pie. We'd like to present it to your cousin," explained Jean. "Is he here?"

"You'll find Job in the woodshed."

Louise and Jean were glad to have an opportunity to speak alone with the caretaker of Highfort. After giving him the pie they jokingly asked if he would do them a favor in return.

"Will I?" he chuckled. "Just ask me **and**

see! I can't remember when I've eaten home-made pie."

"This is a rather peculiar favor," said Louise, smiling. "It concerns your relative Lettie, so I hesitate to ask you."

"You want me to send her packing?"

"Nothing as drastic as that," smiled the Dana girl. "If she should have a caller in the next day or so, or if she should leave the house to meet anyone, will you notify us?"

"Why, sure, that's not much of a favor. You mean a lady caller."

"No, a man," corrected Louise. "He may call himself Mr. Trout."

"I'll be on the lookout for him," the care-taker promised. "Any little thing I can do for you girls will be cheap pay for a good pumpkin pie," he laughed.

Back at Highfort once more, Louise and Jean sought Sonya who was in her room. The girl had been crying and confessed that she was worried by Mrs. Plimpton's accusation. Without telling her what they knew, the sisters advised her not to worry.

"What makes it serious is that Tranley and I do have jewels in our possession," she declared between sobs.

"The Olavu family jewels?" inquired Louise, feeling sure of the answer.

"Yes, I will show them to you soon. And Tranley has said I may tell you the story connected with them," she smiled, drying her eyes.

"We'd love to hear it," Jean cried eagerly.

"First of all, my brother has said you are to be told the great secret connected with this house," their schoolmate confided.

"We're all ears, Sonya," laughed Louise. "Let's hear it."

"Not yet." The girl shook her head regretfully.

"But when? We've waited so long."

"As soon as Mrs. Plimpton leaves I will tell you. I dare not before."

CHAPTER XIX

Hidden Papers

While the Dana girls chatted with Sonya, Miss Dana called in an excited voice to say that the widow had suddenly decided to depart.

"Louise! Jean!" she summoned her nieces. "Can you help pack her car?"

The girls sprang to their feet, fairly racing down the hall.

"Can we?" echoed Jean gaily. "I should say so!"

Sonya and Cora also assisted in lugging Mrs. Plimpton's many boxes and suitcases downstairs. It was with the greatest difficulty that the Dana girls concealed their joy. They hardly dared look at Marybelle, for fear they would give away the secret.

"I can't stand it another day at Highfort," the stout woman complained, but gave no other explanation for her sudden departure.

"I am sorry you feel that way," replied Miss Dana. "We have tried our best to make it pleasant for you."

"*You* have been nice," the widow admitted unwillingly. "It's just that Highfort is my home, and only guests I ask here have a right to come. Oh dear, I'm so upset."

163

She dabbed a handkerchief to her eyes as she climbed into the car, assisted by both Dana girls.

"You haven't seen the last of me!" she warned in final parting. "I'll get a lawyer and then I'll come back. Highfort belongs to me and——"

Marybelle at the wheel started the motor and the car moved away.

"Three rousing cheers!" proposed Jean, dancing a jig in the snow. "She has gone at last."

"For the time being," amended Miss Dana. "I greatly fear she will return to make further trouble."

"Now to hear the story of Highfort!" urged Louise, turning to Sonya. "Are you willing to reveal the secret?"

"Yes," nodded the girl, "let us all gather inside. Here come your uncle and Tranley. Everyone is here now."

Cora was sent to Job Tryon's bungalow upon a pretext, and then the Danas gathered about the living room fireplace to hear the strange story.

"You tell it, Tranley," Sonya urged her brother. "You speak English with more ease than I."

"As you know," began the young man, "this mansion originally was an old fort. That is why this estate on Indian Mountain is called

Highfort. When first the building was constructed for use in war it contained a huge fireplace with steps leading to the roof.''

"I've read about such places!" exclaimed Louise, her eyes alight.

"Similar fireplaces were common in our country long ago. The one here at Highfort through strange circumstances was built by a man who had been a faithful servant in the Olavu family."

"That is certainly most unusual," said Captain Dana.

"The man had been sent to this country on a secret mission," contributed Sonya. "Important papers were sewn into the lining of his clothing."

"This good servant met with misfortune," Tranley resumed the story. "He was attacked by enemies, injured, and left by the roadside. Kind people cared for him, and brought him to their own home, not many miles from here. During his illness many things slipped from the servant's mind, but one important thought remained always with him.

"The papers which he had upon his person must be protected from enemies.

"Later, after he had recovered his health, the servant was given a chance to work on the fort then under construction. In desperation he built a secret compartment into the fireplace and there hid his precious papers."

"All this must have happened many years ago," commented Miss Dana. "How did you learn of it, Tranley?"

"Shortly after the papers had been hidden, the man was injured when a building beam fell on him. Dying, he begged a friend to get word of his act to our family. Years later this was done."

"Then the papers were recovered?" inquired Captain Dana.

"Unfortunately they were not. The Olavus sent an agent to this country to make discreet inquiry. Entrance to the fort could not be gained without permission from the military authorities."

"And such permission would require a full explanation," commented Uncle Ned.

"Yes, sir, that was why the matter was dropped temporarily. Years later information came to us that the fort had been abandoned as a military post. Through a real estate firm our parents were able to purchase the property. They felt that the papers never would be found until a member of the family should come here to claim them."

"And that was what brought you and Sonya to Highfort?" questioned Jean, as she interrupted his narrative.

"Not entirely. When my sister and I were forced to flee from our native land we brought with us valuable jewels. We decided to hide them in the old fireplace at the first opportunity and at the same time recover the papers.''

"These documents—would they still be valuable?" Captain Dana asked dubiously.

"Oh yes, indeed, sir. The records would be of great assistance to unfortunates in our native land today. Through them we might be able to get some aid from your country."

"Tranley and I received what you might call a great shock," Sonya took up the story. "We came here expecting to find a fort. What do we see? A magnificent home with not one owner but three!"

"And to confuse us further, not one of the fireplaces fits the description given us," Tranley continued. "I have examined all of them carefully."

"Since the fort was remodeled, isn't it possible the old fireplace also was rebuilt?" asked Louise quietly.

"Yes, I thought of that same thing," agreed Tranley. "They may have been made smaller. I want to hire workmen and have the new ones torn down so I can examine them further."

"A very natural desire," said Captain Dana. "However, as I represent Mr. Fairweather's interests, I fear I can't give my consent."

"But, sir, we own Highfort."

"Did it ever occur to you that your real estate broker may have tricked you regarding the sale?"

"No, I never thought of that!" Tranley cried, visibly shaken. "Is it possible?"

"I am not saying he did," Uncle Ned declared hastily. "But it could have happened. For that reason it would be unwise to damage the property until you are certain of your claim."

"Then what are we to do?" asked Sonya excitedly. "How are we to recover our papers? Where shall we hide the jewels?"

"I think the safest place for the gems would be a bank vault," declared Louise quickly. "Don't you agree, Uncle Ned?"

"I certainly do," he replied. "If they were mine I'd never trust them to a fireplace."

"I'll take your advice, Captain Dana," Tranley said. "Sonya, will you please bring the jewels from your room?"

His sister returned in a few minutes bearing a large flat case of tooled leather. Across its face in age-mellowed colors appeared the Olavu family coat of arms.

The object was much admired by everyone, and then Sonya lifted the lid. Lying on a velvet pad were rings, sparkling bracelets and necklaces of bright-colored stones.

"Did you ever see anything so lovely?" she asked reverently. "This particular necklace is set with blue-fire diamonds. My great-grandmother wore it on her wedding day."

Sonya dropped the necklace into Louise's lap. Jean moved closer to inspect the jewels. Her eyes met those of her sister. So far as they could tell, the diamonds had no sparkle. They appeared to be cheap glass. But lest their judgment be faulty, they remained silent.

It was Tranley who spoke. "May I see that necklace?" he asked in an agitated voice.

Louise gave it to him and watched his expression eagerly. The young man examined the stones, then his face tightened into grim lines.

"This is not the Olavu necklace!" he announced dramatically. "It is a substitute! We've been robbed!"

CHAPTER XX

THE DETECTIVE

EVERYONE except the Dana girls was stunned by Tranley's announcement. They too would have been startled had they not observed for themselves that the necklace was an imitation.

"Sonya, let me have the other jewels!" cried the young man, taking the case from his sister. "Ah, it is as I feared!"

"All substitutes?" asked Jean soberly.

"Yes, we have been robbed! These are not the Olavu jewels!"

Louise and Jean might have thought that Sonya and her brother never had possessed any valuable gems were it not for the fact that they actually had seen the original diamond star pin. As it was, they did not doubt Tranley's statement; rather, they were led to believe that the two were victims of a plot which reached beyond the boundaries of Highfort.

"Who could have taken away our beautiful pieces?" Sonya murmured brokenly.

"I don't like to say this," said Captain Dana, "but Mrs. Plimpton left Highfort very suddenly. That looks suspicious."

"And she disliked Sonya and me!" exclaimed Tranley. "We might have known——"

"Before you came, Mrs. Plimpton herself was robbed," Louise reminded him.

"The jewel case was in my locked suitcase. Neither Marybelle nor Mrs. Plimpton could have found the key," said Sonya.

"What about this man Fairweather?" Tranley inquired abruptly. "And his chauffeur Jenkins? Perhaps there is a reason why they haven't appeared at the mansion."

"You're not suggesting that they had anything to do with the robbery?" Captain Dana asked in amazement.

"Is it so impossible? They might have learned that my sister had the jewels——"

"Don't you say such mean, cruel things about my Jenkins!"

Tranley was interrupted by Cora Appel who had just returned from her errand and had heard part of the conversation from the doorway. To the consternation of the Danas she darted forward, facing the young man with stormy eyes.

"He's honest, he is, an' he wouldn't steal from anyone! Mr. Fairweather's good and kind, too, and you ain't got no right to blacken their names!"

"Cora!" reproved Miss Dana.

"I don't care—it's the truth. I won't stand by and let 'em abuse my future intended."

"I'm sorry, Cora," Tranley said. "I guess I'm wrong."

Mollified, the maid returned to the kitchen, but for a time she showed her disapproval by banging pots and pans.

"It puzzles me how the substitution was made in the jewels," Louise remarked after a time. "Tell me, Sonya, do these pieces closely resemble the ones which were lost?"

"Yes, they do. I did not notice an exchange had been made until Tranley spoke."

"Wouldn't that suggest the robbery was carefully planned?" Jean asked quickly.

"I was thinking the same thing," nodded Louise. "Someone who had a previous knowledge of the jewels must have made the substitution. The number of pieces is the same, Sonya?"

"Yes, it is. The only change appears to be in the gems," the girl replied.

"Undoubtedly the thief hoped that the substitution would not be discovered so quickly. Sonya, when did you last look at your jewels?"

"Let me think—" The girl's thin eyebrows puckered. "It was the day before Christmas. I am very sure I opened the case while I was dressing to go for the sleigh ride."

"No strangers have called at Highfort since then," remarked Miss Dana.

"Not to our knowledge," suggested Jean.

"Job Tryon comes now and then," Captain Dana reminded them. "Still, I'll stake my command, he's honest."

The affair was discussed from every angle but no conclusions regarding the identity of the thief were reached. Examination did not reveal that Sonya's suitcase had been forced open. The robber must have used a skeleton key.

Louise and Jean had very little to say until they were alone. Then the latter remarked thoughtfully:

"Louise, I suppose this sounds crazy, but I've been wondering if Vitescom may not have something to do with the theft?"

"It's not a crazy idea, Jean. I was thinking the same thing."

"We saw him in town just before Sonya arrived here."

"And his two friends weren't far away," completed Louise. "They could have helped him watch the house for a chance to get inside. He's certainly a person who could have had an accurate knowledge of the Olavu jewels."

"We know Vitescom is a scoundrel. He couldn't get Sonya to give him the gems for his so-called cause, so why shouldn't he steal them?"

"The footprints we found on the rug suggest that the culprit was a man," resumed Louise. "Oh, everything points to Vitescom!"

As the girls excitedly discussed their theory, they thought of many new factors which made it plausible. It was highly logical that Vitescom should follow Sonya and Tranley from Penfield, for he was not the type of person to abandon a blackmail scheme.

"Assuming it was Vitescom, how did he enter Highfort?" mused Louise.

"He might have tried to gain entrance from the roof. I saw someone there, you know. Or else he may have had a key."

"I'm more inclined to think that he had an accomplice right in the house, Jean."

"Mrs. Plimpton?"

"She could have let him into the mansion. The woman seems to have a craving for jewels."

"Having her own gems stolen may have been a blind!" cried Jean as a new thought came to her. "Perhaps she never lost them at all, but merely tried to throw the blame on Sonya and Tranley!"

"And even Marybelle was fooled."

"It would be a clever trick—almost too clever for Mrs. Plimpton. But then, it's possible she deceived us by acting a part. I thought she was queer in the head, but that may have been a pose, too. The fact remains, the woman left Highfort very suddenly."

"Since she was determined to hold the estate at all cost, it does seem strange she would give up so easily," Jean added.

"Maybe," suggested Louise, "the woman wasn't Mrs. Plimpton at all. She could be just a plain thief and a member of some gang!"

The discussion was interrupted as the Dana girls caught a glimpse of Job Tryon approaching the house. Meeting him at the door they learned that he had come to give them a message.

"You said to let you know when Lettie had a caller," he said in a lowered voice. "Well, she's just leaving my place now to meet some fellow. He called her on the phone."

"Who is the man?" asked Louise.

"Didn't hear his name. He claims to be a detective or something. But I don't like it that Lettie is running off to meet him. I wish her father was here, but he went off on some business."

"We'll follow and see that no harm comes to her," the Danas promised.

"That's mighty kind of you, Miss. I'd go myself only with all that's been happening at Highfort, I think I better stay here."

"Which way did Lettie go?" they asked the man as he prepared to leave.

"She said she was driving into town," he replied, starting his car.

"Thanks," called Jean cheerily. "I think we'll be able to overtake her."

She and Louise quickly dressed in heavy garments and set out in the Dana automobile. The roads were slippery, the curves dangerous, but the girls made excellent time. Before they had gone three miles they saw the Briggs' car a short distance ahead.

"Slow down, Jean," Louise advised. "We don't want Lettie to know we're following her."

Unaware that she was being trailed, the girl ahead kept on until she had reached the outskirts of the village. There she drew up in front of a dilapidated, unpainted inn which bore a sign, "Rooms—One Dollar and Up."

Jean stopped the automobile some distance down the road. Even so, she and Louise narrowly escaped detection, for as Lettie alighted she glanced in their direction. The girls hastily ducked down into the bottom of the car where they remained until the other had entered the hotel.

"Shall we risk following her inside?" Jean asked dubiously.

"We must if we're to learn anything."

Not without misgivings the Danas walked into the main lobby of the inn. The room was practically deserted, and they instantly realized that unless they used the utmost caution Lettie would see them. The Briggs girl had presented herself at the desk and was talking to the sleepy-eyed clerk.

"Is Mr. Holweg Trout registered here?" Louise and Jean heard her inquire.

"Yes," the man answered. "You'll find him in the writing room."

After Lettie had left the lobby, her schoolmates wandered as close to the doorway she had entered as they dared. The clerk glanced carelessly at them, but assumed they were waiting for someone.

From inside the writing room came a low mumble of voices. The Dana girls could not understand a word of the conversation, but they noted that the man spoke with a distinct and familiar accent.

"We've heard that voice before!" Jean whispered in her sister's ear.

"He sounds like Vitescom!" nodded Louise. "If only we dare peep in there and make certain!"

CHAPTER XXI

A Wild Ride

So long as the hotel clerk remained in plain view, the Dana girls were afraid to move closer to the doorway. They could not hope to enter the writing room without being observed by Lettie and her detective friend.

"At least we must follow the man when he leaves here," whispered Jean. "I'm sure he's that rascal Vitescom."

Louise nodded and indicated a large, ornate Japanese screen which stood just inside the doorway.

"Jean, if I could get behind that I could see the man plainly."

"It's too dangerous. You'll be detected."

"Not if I'm cautious," insisted Louise, "but we'll take no unnecessary chances. You return to the car and get the engine started. Then, if the man should leave the inn suddenly, you'll be prepared to follow him."

"All right. But do be careful, Louise."

Jean arose and crossed the lobby. While the clerk's attention was drawn away from her, Louise stealthily moved behind the screen. So engrossed were Lettie and the "detective" that they failed to observe her as she glided across the open space.

One glance assured Louise that she and Jean had not been mistaken. The man who talked with Lettie was indeed Vitescom, disguised by a mustache.

Although Louise now stood fairly close to the couple, she could not understand what they were saying. Lettie spoke in a low tone and the man clipped his speech. Only two words did she hear distinctly—"Dana" and "Fairweather." As the couple turned to leave the writing room, however, Lettie laughed and said:

"Oh, don't worry about that. I never fail in my sleuthing."

Louise waited until they had gone, then followed. As she emerged from the hotel she saw that Vitescom was walking swiftly toward a parked car. Lettie had lingered near the building and instantly observed the alert Dana watcher. In panic she tried to signal to Vitescom, but he paid no heed to her call.

"Oh, hello, Louise," she said, trying not to appear flustered. "What in the world are you doing here?"

"Not a thing at present," Louise replied airily. "But I have high hopes."

She had no intention of being delayed, but she did wish to learn certain facts from Lettie. Accordingly, she suggested the girl speak to her sister. As they approached the Dana car, she gave Jean a significant look.

"Won't you ride with us, Lettie?" invited Jean, guessing her sister's meaning.

"No, thanks. I brought my own car."

"Do ride with us," urged Louise, crowding her close to the automobile.

"I'm afraid we must insist, Detective Briggs!" chuckled Jean.

Seizing Lettie's hand she pulled, while Louise gave a quick boost. The girl landed squarely in the seat. Louise sprang in beside her and slammed the door.

"Full speed forward, Jean!" she said tersely. "Follow that car ahead!"

"You can't do this to me!" Lettie protested shrilly. "Let me out or I'll scream!"

"I shouldn't if I were you," advised Louise. "You might find it hard to explain to the police your association with that crook you've just been talking to."

"What crook?" Lettie was shocked. "You don't mean Detective Holweg Trout?"

"Evidently you don't recognize Mr. Vitescom when you see him," Louise said, her eyes scanning the road ahead. "That trick mustache of his must have fooled you."

"You say he's Vitescom? The man who threatened Sonya?"

"The very same. Now will you tell us what you know about him?"

"I—I met him in town," Lettie gasped. "He was so handsome and so polite. He told me he was a friend of the man who owns Highfort. Mr. Fairweather."

"What else?" questioned Jean.

She fed the motor more gasoline for the car ahead had gained headway.

"Well, he said he understood that uninvited guests had taken possession of Highfort. He asked me to learn what I could so he might report to the owner."

"So that was why you were peeping in the window! Did Mr. Vitescom tell you anything about Mr. Fairweather?" asked Louise.

"He asked me a few things about him. Nothing of importance. But he didn't tell me anything."

Louise and Jean had no wish to reveal their own knowledge to Lettie. Nevertheless, they instantly became convinced that the fake detective had played a part in Mr. Fairweather's failure to arrive at the estate. Was it not likely that he had waylaid the car?

"The Olavu family jewels have been stolen," Louise told Lettie severely. "Perhaps Vitescom took them, perhaps he didn't. Be that as it may, you're taking a great risk to associate with such a person."

"I thought he was an honest detective," Lettie half sobbed. "Let me out of the car. Please! I'll get my father to take me home— I'll go away from Highfort and never return."

Not wishing to be burdened with the girl, Jean drew up at the side of the road. Lettie alighted and the auto sped on.

"Now to overtake Vitescom," Louise urged. "We can't let him escape."

The car ahead wound through the countryside and finally turned into a little-used farm road. Try as she would, Jean could not cut down the distance between the two autos.

"Louise, he must know we're following him," she declared as the car skidded around a curve. "He's driving faster and faster."

"Slow down, Jean. Even if he gets away we can't afford to risk a smash-up," advised her sister nervously. "These roads are dangerous."

"I wish we'd pass a state trooper," said the younger girl.

"So do I, but there's not much chance of that on this road."

As the chase carried them deeper into the hills, the girls neither met nor passed anyone who might give them assistance. Although they were able to keep the Vitescom car in view they could not overtake it.

Presently, after the chase had lasted many

miles, the road curled beneath a railroad trestle.
Emerging suddenly from the semi-dark tunnel,
Jean too late saw an empty automobile parked
squarely in the road. She slammed on the foot
brake, but a collision could not be avoided. The
Dana car skidded sideways, crashing into the
left front fender of the other machine.

"Are you hurt, Jean?" Louise asked anxiously, for her sister had slumped against the
steering wheel.

"Just shaken up." With an effort Jean
straightened. "How about you?"

"Jolted a bit, that's all. But we had a close
call. Say, that is Vitescom's car!"

Jean's eyes flashed angrily. "It was left in
the road on purpose. That man deliberately
caused an accident so we couldn't follow him."

Leaving their own car which had been damaged very little, the Dana sisters inspected the
other automobile. There was no sign of an oc-
cupant and no one in sight.

"Where did the fellow go? He couldn't have
vanished into thin air," commented Louise with
a puzzled frown.

"He's hiding somewhere near by, waiting for
us to leave, you may be sure of that."

Although the girls searched in the fields, looking behind trees and bushes, they could find
no trace of the missing man. Fearing that some
other car might have a disastrous crash, they

carefully pushed Vitescom's vehicle to the edge of the road.

"Why don't we drain out all the gasoline?" Jean proposed impulsively. "Then if the rascal does come back he'll not be able to drive away. In the meantime we'll notify the police."

"A good idea except for one thing." Louise smiled ruefully as she inspected the gauge.

"Empty?"

"Dry as a bone. I guess that was why Vitescom abandoned the car."

Rather disgusted with themselves for not having inspected the fuel tank sooner, the girls walked to their own automobile. Louise swung open the door only to stare at a sheet of soiled paper lying on the front seat.

"What's this?" she murmured, picking it up eagerly.

One quick glance at the sheet assured Louise that it was a threatening note. In a bold scrawl had been written the following terse message:

TAKE WARNING. DO NOT FOL-LOW IF YOU EXPECT TO SEE YOUR FAMILY AGAIN.

CHAPTER XXII

A Clue from Penfield

"Vitescom must have written this message!" Louise exclaimed, offering the paper to her sister to read.

"But how was he able to leave it on the car seat?" Jean asked in perplexity. "Why didn't we see him?"

"No doubt he stole to our car while we were searching the fields."

"Where do you suppose Vitescom was hiding?" asked Jean.

"On the railroad bridge. We never thought of looking there."

Quickly the sisters climbed up the embankment following a trail of fresh footprints but the man they sought was nowhere in sight.

"By this time he is probably half a mile down the road," said Louise.

"Let's drive on and see if we can find him," her sister pleaded.

"Ignore the warning?"

"Why not? At least we can find out where he is staying."

"Right you are," agreed Louise as they climbed into the car.

The Dana girls knew that by resuming the pursuit they might be running into danger. Nevertheless, they were determined to go on.

With courage high Jean and Louise followed the narrow road until it joined a main highway two miles farther on. They caught no glimpse of Vitescom, and at length were forced to give up the search. Retracing their way, Jean presently called attention to a narrow side road and a sign which read:

"Harter's Highlands. Three miles."

"Doesn't that name sound familiar, Louise?" the girl asked.

"Yes, it does, but I can't think where I've heard it," her sister added.

"We might investigate the road."

"It's too late now, Jean. The folks will begin to worry about us. Anyway, I'd like to tell them what we've learned and see if they don't think we should notify the police."

This was agreed and the girls sped toward Highfort. Jean mentioned being hungry and suggested stopping for a few minutes to get a bite of food.

The proposal pleased Louise, who kept an alert watch for a roadside restaurant. Soon she saw one ahead and instructed her sister to slow down. As the car drew up before the building, both girls noticed a familiar gray sedan standing not a dozen yards away.

"Why, that looks like Mrs. Plimpton's automobile!" Louise exclaimed, staring.

As she spoke the sisters received a second surprise. From the restaurant came Mrs. Plimpton, talking angrily. Behind her walked Marybelle, Sonya, Tranley and a state trooper.

"Goodness, how did they get here? And what is the argument about?" Jean whispered excitedly.

Without noticing the Dana girls, Mrs. Plimpton protested bitterly to the officer. "This is an outrage! I shall not submit to having my luggage searched! Positively I will not! How dare you suggest that I have stolen jewels in my possession!"

"Sorry, ma'am," the trooper replied, opening the door of the Plimpton car. "The Olavus have made a complaint against you, so it's my duty to make the search."

"Oh, dear, never was I so mortified, so humiliated in all my life!" the widow said brokenly. "I feel faint. Marybelle, my smelling salts! Get them quickly!"

"They're packed in the suitcase, Miss Daisy," answered the maid, slipping a protective arm about her mistress. "Just lean on me."

Louise and Jean stepped from their car and hurried forward eagerly. As the trooper hesitated to begin the task, Tranley became impatient.

"Go right ahead, Officer," he urged. "I'm sure you will find the stolen jewels in the possession of these women."

One by one the suitcases were opened, and the contents carefully examined. Bundles were unwrapped and packages laid bare. The missing Olavu jewels could not be found.

"There, I hope you're satisfied!" Mrs. Plimpton fairly screamed.

"Sorry, but I must ask to see the contents of your purse," the officer said. "Your maid will have to submit to a search too."

Marybelle glanced despairingly at the Dana girls, but they could do nothing to help her. While a group of curious bystanders watched with great interest, the two women were searched. Neither jewels nor pawnbroker receipts were found upon their persons.

"You'll pay for this outrage!" Mrs. Plimpton declared, glaring at Sonya and Tranley. "I'll sue you for damages!"

The Olavus' apology for their mistake was ignored coldly. It was to the Dana girls that the excited widow now turned for sympathy in her distress.

"Don't let this upset you," Louise said soothingly. "Now and then mistakes are made. Will you sit in our car while Marybelle and the officer repack your luggage?"

"Yes, thank you. Such a time," Mrs. Plimpton murmured. She sagged heavily into the car seat. "Why, I never stole anything in all my life!"

Jean and Louise changed the subject by talking of Highfort. Adroitly they questioned the widow, asking if she knew what remodeling work originally had been done upon the mansion.

"No, I don't," Mrs. Plimpton answered shortly. "My husband took charge of it and told me nothing."

"You never heard if the fireplaces were rebuilt?" probed Louise, looking intently at the woman.

"No, and what's more, if I did know I wouldn't tell you a thing!" Mrs. Plimpton said unpleasantly. "You're always asking questions and it annoys me!"

The Dana girls wisely asked no additional ones, but they casually mentioned the name of Vitescom in their conversation with each other. Even the remark that the man was interested in Highfort brought not the slightest change of expression upon the widow's face. Presently they tried out Holweg Trout but this brought no sign of recognition.

The trooper soon finished repacking the luggage. At a nod from him Mrs. Plimpton awkwardly alighted from the Dana car. Without a word of good-bye she entered her own automobile and drove away.

Sonya and Tranley looked very downcast as

they came to talk with Louise and Jean. The Danas were afraid their schoolmate was going to cry.

"We made a mistake, I guess," the young man admitted. "I was sure Mrs. Plimpton had our jewels or I never would have followed her here and insisted upon the search."

"We do what you call put our foot in it," added Sonya ruefully. "Now the widow will try to make trouble for us."

"I hope I didn't make a similar mistake in regard to Vitescom," Tranley said, frowning thoughtfully.

The Dana girls were startled by the young man's mention of the familiar name. Questioned, he readily explained that at Sonya's request he had asked for the man's arrest.

"Is it not possible that he took our jewels?" the girl asked gravely. "You told me you were sure you had seen him once in this very village."

"Jean and I saw the man less than an hour ago," Louise revealed. "He can't be very far from here right now."

She then disclosed how Vitescom had eluded capture by deserting his car.

"That's important information," declared Tranley eagerly. "I'll tell the officer and have him resume the search."

The trooper had gone into the restaurant to telephone to headquarters. Tranley found him there, and after a brief conversation with the man returned to the Dana car.

"He promises to look for Vitescom," young Olavu told the girls, "but he did not seem very enthusiastic. Since the jewels weren't found in Mrs. Plimpton's car, he distrusts me."

Louise slipped into the building and asked the trooper if any word had come from or about Mr. Fairweather. Upon a negative reply, she told the officer some of her suspicions and he promised to report everything and suggest that the search be intensified.

Tranley was discouraged by his failure to recover the lost gems. He brightened, however, when Jean said she thought they all should return to Highfort, there to make a thorough inspection of the premises.

"Even if the jewels are gone, it's still possible to find the family papers secreted in the old fireplace," she declared cheerfully.

"Possible," Tranley agreed, "but already I have searched without success."

At the mansion once more, Captain Dana joined the young people in their task. With Tranley he climbed to the roof of the building but a careful inspection did not disclose unused chimneys or ancient flues.

"The only thing to do is to tear down the fireplaces," declared the young man. "You will not give your consent, Captain?"

"Well, I don't know," the older man replied

reluctantly. "You really should wait until Mr. Fairweather arrives."

"But we may never see him again."

"I can't believe that," returned Captain Dana. "However, I'll agree to this. If Fairweather doesn't come by tomorrow you may tear down the fireplaces, provided you'll pay for any damage you may do to them."

"I should expect to—if your friend's claim to the property is a valid one."

While the two men were discussing the work to be done, Job Tryon arrived at the fortress home bearing mail. Among the letters was one which surprised them. It was from Mrs. Crandall, addressed to Louise and Jean.

"What does she say?" the latter inquired absently as her sister scanned the communication.

"Listen to this, Jean! Mrs. Crandall writes that a young man by the name of Cordell Wayland has been arrested at Penfield."

"Never heard of him."

"Why, Jean, he's an assistant to that Mr. Goldman!"

"The Penfield pawnbroker?"

"Yes, and this is the important part. Wayland recently admitted that he had substituted fake jewels for genuine ones pawned in the shop. One of the pieces was a star pin of diamonds."

"Belonging to Sonya!"

"Of course. For doing the job he was given three hundred dollars by a man who called himself V. Holweg."

"Holweg—" Jean repeated in a startled voice. "Sounds like Holweg Trout!"

"And Holweg Trout is Mr. Vitescom! Oh, now more than ever we must bring about that fellow's capture," said Louise excitedly.

"Easier said than done. So far Mr. Vitescom has proven more than a match for us."

"We know he was somewhere near Harter's Highland today."

"Say that name again, Jean," Louise said in a tense voice.

"Harter's Highland?"

"Jean, I have it!" Springing to her feet, Louise paced excitedly across the room.

"Have what?"

"Jean, don't you get it? Hunter's Island sounds almost like Harter's Highland!"

"Why, it does! Over a telephone they could sound exactly alike. Could Mr. Vitescom have been on his way there when we followed him?" her sister asked excitedly.

"That would be my guess, Jean. He may be holding Mr. Fairweather a prisoner in a dark den." Louise's eyes danced with excitement. "Furthermore, maybe the stolen jewels are cached there—for all we know in the so-called mysterious fireplace!"

CHAPTER XXIII

A New Theory

In the light of their latest theory many hitherto unexplained matters suddenly seemed clear. Convinced that Mr. Fairweather and Jenkins were being held prisoners somewhere near Harter's Highland, the Dana girls startled the household by their demand that an immediate search be made.

"There may be something to the idea!" Captain Dana exclaimed. "At least it's worth an investigation. I'll organize a searching party at once."

"May Jean and I go along?" Louise pleaded. "Please don't say 'no.'"

"Yes, you deserve the right," their uncle nodded. "But dress warmly for we may be out all night."

While Captain Dana telephoned for state troopers to meet him at a designated place, Aunt Harriet helped the girls prepare for the trip. It had already grown dark and the temperature was dropping steadily.

Tranley brought the car to the door, and to his surprise Sonya, clad in furs, stepped into it.

194

"I am going along," she announced calmly. "I shall not accept 'no' for an answer."

A half hour later the Dana car was met at Blakeman's Crossroad by two state troopers, Fuller and Marsh.

"We'll drive first to the village of Harter's Highland," the latter told the group. "Maybe I can pick up a little information from the townsfolk."

With snow beating against the windshield, the Dana car followed the troopers' automobile over the icy hills. A stop was made at Harter's Highland, a town of less than one hundred inhabitants. Trooper Fuller made inquiry at a gasoline station, while Louise and Jean accosted a woman who chanced to be passing. She said that she had not seen anyone answering the description of Vitescom, Fairweather or Jenkins.

She was sure that she would have if they were around, since her husband was a lumberman and through him she kept pretty good track of newcomers.

"For all I know, they could have passed this way," she disclosed. "These last few days there's been a lot of traffic on the old mill road."

"Where does the mill road lead?" queried Louise before the woman could walk on.

"Nowhere except to a summer colony that's supposed to be closed up now. It's on the edge of a small lake."

"Do the houses have telephones?"

"In summertime. But the place is empty now. Seems kinda funny so many folks have been drivin' in and out."

When Trooper Fuller returned he agreed with the Danas that the new clue should be investigated. Well acquainted with the locality, he led the way along the bumpy, frozen mill road. Captain Dana steered cautiously and strained his eyes trying to keep the tail light of the other car in sight, as the auto wound around curve after curve.

"Slow down, Uncle Ned," Louise presently warned. "I think Trooper Fuller is stopping."

Both cars halted at the side of the road. The policemen alighted. Fuller, coming to speak with Captain Dana, waved his hand vaguely toward the right.

"The first of the summer places is over there somewhere—two or three hundred yards from this road."

"One can't see a thing," the captain complained. "Have you a lantern, or don't we dare use it?"

"It's safer to approach without a light. Can't tell what we may run into."

Warning the members of his party to keep close together and make no noise, the trooper led the way across a deep, frozen ditch. After considerable difficulty he came upon a trail which had been made in the snow and which wound through the trees. Soon a summer cottage loomed up a short distance ahead. Its windows were dark and there was no sign that the house was occupied.

"Looks like another false alarm—" the policeman began, only to break off.

From somewhere near the house a dog had begun to bark. The animal could be heard padding toward them.

"Keep back!" Trooper Fuller ordered the girls. "I may have to wrestle the animal if he proves to be ferocious."

"The noise would warn of our approach," said Louise. "Why can't we split up the party?" she suggested quickly. "Some of us can stay here to distract the dog, while the others approach the house from a different route. In that way if the place is guarded we may fool the lookouts."

The plan was adopted immediately. Louise, Jean, Captain Dana and Fuller circled the house, leaving Sonya, Tranley and Marsh behind.

All went well until the four in the lead were near the house.

Then suddenly Louise, who brought up the rear of the line, gave a cry of alarm. As the others turned to look back, they were horrified to see her vanishing as if into the ground.

"Help!" came her muffled call. "I've tumbled into a great, deep hole!"

The hole proved to be a shallow well, and fortunately there was no water in it. Louise had landed on her feet and was not hurt. Nevertheless, it required the combined strength of Captain Dana and the trooper to pull her out.

"Listen!" warned Jean nervously. "Here comes that dog again!"

The huge animal bounded through the hedge. He began to growl, and from inside the darkened dwelling another dog answered.

"We've given ourselves away now!" muttered Captain Dana in disgust.

The watchdog would have attacked the party had not Trooper Fuller and Captain Ned caught and tied the dog securely. Knowing that a quiet approach was now impossible, the four investigators walked boldly to the front door of the summer home.

The policeman pounded on the heavy panel with his fist. At first there was no indication of occupants within.

"We heard a dog barking from inside only a moment ago," Louise declared, glancing toward the upstairs windows. "Why don't we break in?"

"We can't just break into a place for that reason," smiled Fuller. "We must have some evidence that——"

"Listen!" commanded Captain Dana. "I thought someone called just then!"

The trooper pressed his ear to the door. "I

do hear a voice very faintly!" he exclaimed.
"Can't make out the words!"

Captain Dana rapped again and shouted:

"Hello! Are you Thomas Fairweather?"

"Yes," came the weak response. "We can't
let you in—prisoners."

The rest was lost but the searchers had heard
enough. The words spurred the men to action.
Unable to force the door, Captain Dana and the
trooper found a heavy ram which they used to
smash a panel in it. All the while there was
loud barking and savage growls from within.

"Watch out for the dog!" the officer instructed as they entered the dark dwelling and
played a flashlight around.

Before an investigation could be made it was
necessary to subdue the hound which had been
left to guard the prisoners. Fuller and the captain gave the animal the same treatment the
other dog had received.

"Thomas Fairweather!" Captain Ned Dana
shouted eagerly. "Where are you?"

"Here!" came the muffled reply. "In the
den!"

The searchers found the right door at last.
It was locked and well barricaded from the
outside.

"We'll have you out in a minute, Fairweather!" encouraged Captain Dana.

Unable to open the door by ordinary methods, the men rammed it as they had the outside

one. Captain Dana's flashlight revealed his friend and the chauffeur lying on the leather couches. They were tightly bound. Haggard, unshaven, they staggered to their feet as soon as they were released.

"You've come at last!" Mr. Fairweather murmured, walking feebly to the other room. "Jenkins and I had given up hope."

"Who imprisoned you here?" Captain Dana asked angrily. "Who was the scoundrel?"

"A man named Vitescom."

"Vitescom!" cried Jean Dana triumphantly. "Then our suspicions were correct, Louise! We thought he had a hand in this!"

"Where's the fellow now?" demanded the trooper.

"He and his friends Jack Thorne and Pete Rinner left the premises this morning," Fairweather explained. "They come and go."

The two men were led to the living room where Captain Dana built a fire in the grate. The trooper went to speak to the other members of the party and make plans with Marsh for Vitescom's capture should the man return. The Olavus excitedly came to the house. As everyone listened intently, Mr. Fairweather and his servant told their story.

Upon taking leave of the Danas, they had journeyed toward Highfort. Halfway there they had been stopped by Vitescom who claimed that his car had broken down. He had requested a lift, explaining that he was traveling toward Indian Mountain.

"You weren't suspicious, Mr. Fairweather?" asked Louise at a pause in the narrative.

"Not at first. The fellow told us he had rented a house not far from Highfort and that he intended to bring an invalid sister there for a rest cure."

"He claimed to know the way to the estate," contributed Jenkins. "Said he'd visited the place many times, and that he'd be glad to point out the road to us."

"You trusted him to guide you?" Captain Dana asked.

"Foolishly, we did," nodded Mr. Fairweather. "We never suspected a thing until we drove into the road to this place. Then as Jenkins and I were protesting, two men stepped out of some bushes. They strong-armed us, put on gags and dragged us to this house. We've been held here ever since."

"Did they mistreat you?" asked Captain Dana.

"We slept most of the time," said Jenkins.

"They made me write a note to you and our meals were poor," added Tom Fairweather. "We were entertained by their bickering. From conversation we overheard I'm sure they are planning a big deal which involves Highfort. That was why they didn't want me to be there. If they had known you Danas were going to the place, you probably would have been kidnaped too.'

"The big deal you mention already has been accomplished," said Jean ruefully. "A valuable collection of jewels has disappeared."

"Jewels? At Highfort?"

"A great deal has happened since you were imprisoned," explained Louise, and briefly told of the claims of the Olavus and the woman calling herself Mrs. Plimpton. "Jean and I believe the gems must have been stolen by Vitescom or his accomplices."

"You may be right," said Mr. Fairweather in an excited voice. "I think you are! But I doubt if any woman was involved."

Before Louise could ask if he had any knowledge of the missing jewels, Jean made inquiry regarding the mysterious telephone call received by Job Tryon.

"Yes, I phoned him," Mr. Fairweather responded. "On Christmas Eve Thorne and Rinner were in the house making merry. They became careless and left the door of the den unlocked. Jenkins and I weren't able to escape from the house, but we did get to the phone. Fortunately it was working. The connection was a poor one and before I could say much to Job they caught me."

"The caretaker thought he understood you to mention a mysterious fireplace," declared Louise eagerly. "Was that right?"

"Yes. I don't fully understand it myself. One night I heard Vitescom remark to his companions, 'Those Dana girls are very smart, but they will never find this place nor the treasure in the fireplace!'"

"Then the jewels must be hidden here in this house!" Louise stared at the hearth before her eyes. "Gracious! And we've built a fire on it!"

Captain Dana moved toward the fireplace, intending to put out the flames. Before he could do so, a long, low whistle came from outside the window.

"That must be one of the troopers!" exclaimed Louise, reaching to extinguish the flashlight. "He's warning us that someone is coming!"

CHAPTER XXIV

The Mysterious Fireplace

EVERYONE waited tensely in the darkened room, expecting that Vitescom and his cohorts were returning to the house. Instead, the visitor proved to be a burly lumberman, husband of the talkative woman previously interviewed by the Dana girls at Harter's Highlands.

"Hello," he shouted, flashing a light through the hall window. "Anyone in there?"

The Danas and their companions, who had put out the fire, remained absolutely quiet and were not seen. They were relieved that the man failed to note the smashed door panel. After muttering to himself, he finally went away.

"We're rid of him," remarked the captain in relief. "It's just as well strangers don't learn what we are about tonight or Vitescom may be warned."

As soon as they were sure the lumberman had left the vicinity, the group again discussed the hiding of the Olavu jewels.

"So our valuables may be hidden in this very fireplace!" exclaimed Tranley, flashing a light over the cobblestone structure. "It won't take long to find out."

204

A careful investigation was made, each one taking a turn, but no secret niche could be found.

"Vitescom couldn't have meant this place. Why don't we drive to Highfort?" Louise suggested at last. "I have a feeling the fireplace we're after is there, not here."

"Besides, Mr. Fairweather and Jenkins are very tired," added Jean.

The troopers were left at the house to watch for the kidnaper and his accomplices. The others crowded into the Dana car.

"My automobile was stolen by one of Vitescom's friends," Mr. Fairweather explained ruefully. "I was stripped of my watch, too, and all my money."

Jean and Louise told of the cheap jewelry one of the men had been seen purchasing in the department store where the fire had occurred. They wondered if it could have been used in the substitution of the Olavu gems.

"I think not," said Tranley. "But probably it was to be used for some other robbery."

During the swift ride to Highfort, the Danas revealed to Mr. Fairweather further information regarding the strange mix-up which had developed about the ownership of the property.

"If only I recover the stolen jewels, I'll be willing to waive my claim," Tranley remarked. "All I ask of Highfort is that it give up the Olavu family papers supposedly secreted there."

Upon reaching the estate, Mr. Fairweather and Jenkins ate a hearty meal and went at once to bed. The others sat up for many hours, excitedly discussing plans. Dawn streaked the eastern sky before Louise and Jean finally went upstairs to their rooms. However, they were abroad by nine o'clock the next morning, eager to work on the remaining points of the mystery.

At breakfast Tranley revealed that Mr. Fairweather was willing to have the necessary walls torn down in a search for the ancient fireplace with the secret niches. Rather than have curious townspeople ask questions, the young people decided to do the work themselves.

All morning the mansion resounded with hammering. Plaster dust filled the rooms as the various small fireplaces were examined. In the living room even the hearth was torn up. Feverishly Tranley pounded and wrecked, but could discover nothing of interest beneath it.

"I'm completely discouraged," he announced at lunch time. "We've done a great deal of damage and to no purpose."

Cora, happy now that Jenkins was safe, had prepared an excellent meal and made special dishes for the victims of the kidnapers. The delicious food went far toward reviving the weary workers.

"Let's not give up yet," said Louise. "Instead, why not apply brains instead of brawn to the problem?"

"We'll turn the job over to you," laughed Jean as the group returned to the living room. "You tell us where to find the old fireplace and we'll do the work."

"I've been thinking—" said Louise slowly. "You recall those strange footprints we discovered in the living room?"

"The ones which went to the wall and never returned?" asked her sister.

"Yes, and then we found our Christmas tree upset," the other mused.

"What are you hinting?" Jean asked impatiently. "We've already tapped the wall on that side of the room. It was solid as a rock, don't you remember?"

"I know, but I still think the intruder——"

Jumping to her feet, Louise crossed the room and once again tapped the wall opposite the fireplace. It gave off no hollow sound.

"You see—" Jean began, only to lapse into silence.

Louise had dropped to her knees and was examining the floor. The rug had been rolled to one side to keep it clean.

"Nothing but the usual planks," observed Tranley in disappointment. "No trapdoor or anything of the sort."

"This board seems loose." With trembling hands Louise jerked at it.

So suddenly did it give, along with a whole section, that she tumbled backward. The young people did not laugh. They were staring into a dark cavity which had been revealed.

"I see steps leading down!" cried Tranley excitedly. "We must investigate at once."

The shouts of the young people brought the entire household. Applecore, upon peering down into the deep hole, pleaded with the Dana girls not to venture into it.

"Nonsense," said Jean undismayed.

"Have a care," warned Miss Dana anxiously from above. "That dreadful man Vitescom may be hiding down there."

"We'll be more than a match for him if he is," replied Louise.

With only a flashlight to guide them, they cautiously descended the stairway, which led to the original floor of the fort. Tranley, who was ahead, suddenly gave a shout of pleasure.

"Here it is! The old fireplace!"

"And with steps in the side leading probably to the roof!" cried Louise. "Only the top of the chimney was closed off at some time. That's why we couldn't look down into it."

The ancient fireplace was a crude affair made of field stone. Immediately it was clear to Jean and Louise that when the fort had been turned into a home, newly constructed floors and walls had completely hidden the old fireplace. The steps leading from the living room and the section of loose flooring under the edge of the rug probably had been little used until lately.

"Our search is at an end!" cried Tranley, fairly beside himself with joy. "Now to find the Olavu papers!"

"And our stolen jewels," Sonya added breathlessly. "Oh, will they be here? I can't bear it if they're gone."

CHAPTER XXV

Holiday's End

While Sonya held the flashlight, Tranley and the Dana girls eagerly examined the ancient fireplace. Almost at once they discovered that someone recently had dug in the soft earth close to the hearth.

"We're too late!" exclaimed Tranley. "That rascal Vitescom has been here ahead of us!"

"We feel sure he came," said Louise quietly, "but that doesn't prove he found the papers. It's my hope he merely hid the jewels in this place."

Taking new heart, Tranley hastened upstairs for digging implements. Without waiting for him to return, Louise and Jean began removing loose dirt with their hands.

"I don't believe anything has been hidden here after all," Louise said in disappointment. "This hole seems to be very shallow."

Jean's exploring fingers had encountered a small, loose stone in the front of the fireplace. She pulled it out. There in a dark cavity was a small tin box.

"I've found something!" she cried triumphantly. "It is heavy, too."

Jean lifted the lid. Inside the box lay a heap of glittering jewels—the star diamond pin, ruby rings, beautiful necklaces and costly antique bracelets.

"It is the Olavu collection!" cried Sonya, fairly overcome by joy. "Let us go quickly and show them to my brother!"

"Not yet," laughed Jean. "Our search isn't finished," she added.

Just then Tranley came clattering down the steps with a spade and a pick-axe.

"Is it not wonderful?" Sonya greeted him. "These clever girls have recovered all our jewels!"

The young man's joy was beyond bounds.

"I hope we're clever enough to find the missing papers," said Louise seriously. "That job may not be so easy."

During the next half hour the young people examined every inch of the ancient fireplace. They were becoming discouraged when Tranley pushed against a stone and felt it move.

"The secret niche!" he shouted. "I've found it!"

Removing the rock, the young man thrust his arm into the cavity and brought out a clay box in the shape of a cylinder.

"The papers should be inside this!" he cried triumphantly.

Tranley's prediction proved to be a correct one. When the lid was removed from the box, a roll of paper, protected by a leather covering, fell into the young man's hand.

"Everything will be what you call fine and dandy now!" laughed Sonya as the happy young people carried their treasures upstairs. "We have our jewels and the precious papers!"

"If only Vitescom were captured it would be perfect," added Louise. "I'll never feel satisfied until that man and his accomplices are behind bars."

"We know now that he must have been V. Holweg, the man who bribed the Penfield pawnbroker's helper," remarked Jean thoughtfully.

Captain Dana and Aunt Harriet were as delighted as their nieces that the jewels and the Olavu papers had been recovered. With Mr. Fairweather safe, they declared there was no further excuse for them remaining at Highfort. The state troopers would take care of the arrests.

"I am anxious to get home," the captain declared. "We'll pack our bags today and be ready for an early morning start."

Louise and Jean were sorry to leave the estate, particularly before Vitescom's capture. They made no protest, however, realizing that soon it would be time for them to return to their boarding school.

"I wish we could stay just one more day," Louise complained to her sister as they prepared for bed that night. "I have a feeling that

Vitescom may return here for the jewels.''

''Especially after he finds out that Mr. Fair-weather and Jenkins were set free,'' remarked Jean. ''Say, what if he should come tonight?''

''No one would be watching for him. He'd escape!'' cried Louise.

Rather dismayed by this possibility, the girls decided that something must be done at once. Dressing quietly they went to the storeroom for a rope and then descended the secret stair-way to the hidden fireplace.

''We may have a long vigil,'' Jean said with a yawn. She sat down with her back to the wall. ''I'm going to try to stay awake,'' she added, her eyes blinking.

As she dozed off a few moments later, Louise nudged her. Someone could be heard coming down the steps.

The Dana girls had their rope ready. As a figure reached the bottom of the stairway, they looped their lasso over his head and shoulders, drawing the knot tight.

''Hey! Let me go!'' he shouted.

''Tranley!'' gasped Jean, for she recognized his voice. ''We thought you were Vitescom!''

''No such luck,'' he rejoined, laughing un-easily. ''I wish I could lay hands on that rascal.''

''What is wrong?'' inquired Louise. ''You seem to be upset about something.''

''I am. I spent the early part of the night

examining those papers we found today. One
—the most important of all—is missing.''

"You came here to search for it?"

"Yes, it must be hidden under some of the
fireplace stones," he said. After a pause he
added, "Unless Vitescom has stolen it!"

Jean and Louise aided the young man in his
search, but the lost paper could not be found.
They were interrupted by hearing Miss Dana
call excitedly from above that her nieces were
not in their room.

"Never worry about Jean and me," Louise
laughed, emerging from the lower chamber.
"We were just examining the ancient fireplace
again."

Before the girls could return to their beds,
an automobile drew up to the door of the mansion. Out jumped Troopers Fuller and Marsh,
who marched a third man between them.

"It's Vitescom!" cried Louise, who had
darted to a window. "They've captured him!
Oh, isn't it wonderful?"

The prisoner was brought into the living room
by the policemen. They explained that the man
had been captured when he attempted to re-
enter the summer home he had rented near
Harter's Highlands. He had denied his identity
but it was now quickly revealed, as Sonya and
the other members of the household assembled.

"Were any papers found in his possession?"
asked Tranley.

"Only this." Trooper Fuller carelessly tossed a yellow sheet on a table.

"Only that!" young Olavu laughed shakily as he seized the paper. "The very one I need."

Speaking rapidly to Vitescom in his own tongue, he demanded to know where the sheet had been obtained. The man sullenly refused to say, but when told that the others had been recovered in the ancient fireplace, he admitted having found the one there in a secret niche. He had planned to hunt further for the rest.

Vitescom's story, translated by Tranley, was to the effect that for many years he had known the Olavu family secret. Without telling anyone, he had paid several visits to the deserted mansion, searching for the mysterious fireplace. It was upsetting to find so many people arriving. He revealed that Mrs. Plimpton was not a cohort.

Learning that Tranley and Sonya were en route to Highfort, he shrewdly guessed that they would carry with them the famous Olavu jewels. Having seen the collection many times in his own country, it was a comparatively easy matter for him to have a duplicate set made to substitute whenever he might get a chance to make the exchange.

"So it was Vitescom who kept trying to get everyone except the Olavus away from Highfort!" commented Louise. "He must have been the one who stole Mrs. Plimpton's jewels."

"Yes," nodded Tranley. "The second time he was trying to take something she nearly caught him. To elude her, he climbed out a window to the roof. You Dana girls nearly caught him, but he escaped."

"And the footprints on the rug? Of course he made them," said Louise.

"He left them unwittingly when he crossed the room to descend to the hidden chamber. Also, he upset the Christmas tree coming out of his hiding place one night."

"What about the warning note in the Christmas stocking?" inquired Jean.

"Vitescom wrote it and also the one left in your car. He escaped along the railroad track."

By questioning the thief further, the girls were able to clear up the entire mystery. The man admitted that he had tried to wrest the fake diamond star pin from Jean on the night of the school entertainment. His reason for accosting her was that he had feared the substitution might be discovered, thus revealing the entire scheme to Tranley and Sonya Olavu.

Although much of the guilt was pinned squarely upon Vitescom, Thorne and Rinner came in for their share of the kidnaping episode. They were caught and jailed as accomplices of the man they called Brains, who had given them the idea of substituting cheap jewelry for valuable pieces.

The legal tangle involving the ownership of

Highfort could not be straightened out so easily. The matter finally was settled after it was found Mrs. Plimpton had no claim. Mr. Fairweather paid the Olavus an additional sum of money and the young man withdrew title, leaving Uncle Ned's old friend in full possession.

One day, shortly after Jean and Louise had returned to school, they received a letter from the jolly man. He cordially invited not only them, but Sonya and Tranley as well, to spend a week-end at the mansion of Highfort.

"I've remodeled the place again," he wrote, "tearing out the sections which hid the old fireplace. Everything is in perfect order and I can promise you a quiet time."

"I fear Mr. Fairweather doesn't understand our natures very well!" smiled Louise.

"Not if he thinks we prefer a *quiet* vacation to an exciting one," added Jean with a chuckle. "Given a choice, we'd choose mystery any time, wouldn't we?"

She spoke the truth, but did not go far enough. She should have said the Dana girls never let an opportunity to solve one go by. Within a short time they were to recognize a chance in "The Clue of the Rusty Key."

"Until another case comes along, let's spend our so-called quiet days right here at Starhurst," said Louise, and Jean nodded in agreement.